# I've Got Sumthin' to Tell Ya

## Written by Keith Coachman

Based on the book *Lost in the Sins of Their Mother*

PublishAmerica
Baltimore

© 2005 by Keith Coachman.

All rights reserved. No part of this book may be reproduced, stored in a retrieval system or transmitted in any form or by any means without the prior written permission of the publishers, except by a reviewer who may quote brief passages in a review to be printed in a newspaper, magazine or journal.

First printing

ISBN: 1-4137-7416-4
PUBLISHED BY
PUBLISHAMERICA, LLLP.
www.publishamerica.com
Baltimore

Printed in the United States of America

This book is dedicated to the three women
I have admired the most in life.

They have been strength in times of weakness.
They have been knowledge in times of uncertainty.
They have been shoulders in time of need.

And their love grows stronger.

To Patti Cake, Dottie Bug, and Gail.
I am grateful to you.

## Table of Contents

| | | |
|---|---|---|
| From the Writer | | 7 |
| Chapter One | To My Daughters | 13 |
| Chapter Two | My First Love | 19 |
| Chapter Three | Maxwell Jackson | 32 |
| Chapter Four | Your Daddy | 45 |
| Chapter Five | The Lord Giveth, the Lord Taketh Away | 56 |
| Chapter Six | Back in the Saddle | 75 |
| Chapter Seven | 'Til Death Do Us Part | 83 |
| Chapter Eight | My First Real Job | 98 |
| Chapter Nine | 104 Lee Street | 104 |
| Chapter Ten | Misguided by Flesh | 113 |
| Chapter Eleven | We All Run from Something | 120 |
| Chapter Twelve | The "Golden" Years | 128 |

## *From the Writer*

THOUGH I SELDOM REMEMBER WHAT I dream, this wasn't the first time my grandmother had visited me in my sleep. In fact, over the three years since her death, she came to me on several occasions urging me to write another book—*her* book. The dreams were rather short, but each time I woke up with a haunting desire to get back to my computer. At first, the dreams were subtle messages that told me that my mom, my aunt, and I had done OK with the first book. When my grandmother would stand in front of me, smile, place her two thumbs up and gesture towards her chest, she was telling me it was time for me to write her side of the story. Then, the dream I had that late April night was so vivid that I actually woke myself up trying to cry out but no air would leave my throat. Even today, I remember everything so vividly it is as if it is a memory from yesterday instead of a dream from so many months ago.

I was on my way to meet my friend and her husband to see if they might need any of the clothes I was taking to the Goodwill Store that day. She arrived at the grove of oranges she loved so much, a bit earlier than her husband did, and it gave us a chance to talk for a while. But, instead of the usual balls of green, yellow, or orange fruits one might expect, the limbs were all hanging heavy with vine-like flowers. She roped some of the vines together, fashioning a kind of crown from the flowers and laid it on her head. I was telling her how much like Jesus she looked and I took her picture so as to remember it always. When her husband finally arrived, the three of us spoke for a bit. I noticed he wasn't looking at any of the clothes I had brought. When I asked if he wanted any of them, he turned to me with the oddest smile on his face.

"No, I don't need them anymore," was all he said.

As I put the last of the boxes back into the trunk of the car, I offered to go and get us all something to drink. I drove to the top of a very steep hill, turned left at the traffic light, drove down the long road to what I thought was a store. I turned into the parking area, which, at a glance, with the grounds covered with fine gravel, took on the appearance of white sand. The older looking building looked as if it were once an ice-cream parlor that, for whatever reason, had been painted solid white, windows included. Instead of getting out to get the drinks as I had intended, I just drove around the building and headed back toward the road.

As I was leaving the driveway, I remember trying to pull up the incline onto the street where several lanes of traffic flowed in each direction. Try as I may, I couldn't give the car the amount of gas it needed, so I sat and thought for a minute, wondering what to do. I couldn't just sit there, so I placed my feet on the ground, lifted the car up, and sat it down on the road facing a direction that would lead me back to where my friends were waiting for me. They were about to leave as I drove up and I barely had enough time to say good-bye. As I watched them drive away, I thought about the house I had just left and was compelled to head back up that steep hill, left at the light, and back towards the whitewashed building that, by now, I had decided must be someone's home.

Once again, I pulled into that gravel driveway. Only this time

## I'VE GOT SUMTHIN' TO TELL YA

I parked, got out, and walked toward the front door. Upon entering the house, it suddenly dawned on me that my brother and his wife had just bought this house and happened to be moving in that day; even though the old white-haired man who had been living there had not moved out yet. It was the same white-haired man we had all seen at the hospital the week my grandmother died! He was waiting for me and he smiled as I entered through the glass doorway, crossing a floor made of different shapes and sizes of red bricks. As I continued through the area that once hosted an ice-cream freezer, a couple of café tables and an old cash register sitting on white Formica counters, I heard some commotion in a room off to the left.

I walked into what looked like the kitchen and was surprised to find my younger sister and my uncle cooking in what is best described as a wood-burning stove. They were laughing hysterically, even though she was getting upset because the oven was not warm enough. My sister's laughs mixed with a childlike whine that only she can get away with, and she kept saying that the food in the oven was not cooking. My uncle was laughing so much that he could not answer her so she turned and asked me what to do. I knew my mom would know how to use a wood-burning stove, so I found the phone and called her. Mom was explaining to me how the stove should work, and as I opened the lower part where the fire should have been, all I found was a stack of white rags cut from some old dress shirts that smelled like kerosene, but had never been lit. My sister opened a door directly beside it and the flames and heat swarmed out towards me. I told Mom that there was plenty of fire, and I opened another door that turned out to be the oven. Only, it wasn't directly beside the fire. Instead, it was on top of a cabinet that sat beside the stove. I opened the door slowly, and as I put my hand in, I cracked up laughing, telling my mom, "Never mind! I found the problem!"

My sister was cooking a frozen pack of corn and a frozen pack of mixed vegetables, both of which were in boil-in-bags. She had them both lying on top of yet another stack of white rags made from old torn dress shirts. I hung up the phone, left my sister and uncle alone to finish cooking, and walked outside. That familiar old white-haired man was warming himself in the sun, looking more like the old man in the sea than I remembered. The folding chair he sat in was also familiar, though I had not seen the like in many years. It was made of thin pipes of gray aluminum, with alternating green and white mesh strips crisscrossing each other to make the seat and back, and had long, white plastic armrests.

He asked what I had been doing lately and seemed very interested as I told him I had written a book with my mom and my aunt. I told him the story about a woman who had raised her two daughters so very poorly and how it had turned out to be very traumatic for both of them and how it ended up molding the rest of their lives. The old man was looking right at me, listening intently to every word I said as, holding back tears, I described how the woman may have caused the death of her first daughter and had definitely killed the two little girls' daddy. I started choking as the tears flowed from my eyes and as I stopped to regain my composure, I noticed that two of my nephews had stopped playing and were sitting next to me listening to everything. Just as I was describing to him that what made our book even more interesting was that it is a true story, I noticed the old man was glancing over my shoulder.

I looked up to see my grandmother standing over me, and I stopped talking. She had evidently been standing there for some time listening to everything I was saying. She just leaned down, wrapped her arms around my neck, and gave me a very firm hug. Then, she kissed me on the cheek, stood up and said to my nephews, "Come on, boys, let's finish playing in the grass so he can finish his story."

She never disputed anything I said. It was as though she wanted me to tell the story, but she did not want her great-grandchildren to hear it, so as not to change how they felt about her. She didn't get upset; she just took the boys off to a grassy area and played with them, as if she wanted them to remember her when the grass was greener.

That is when I woke up, not breathing and trying hard to scream. I swallowed hard one good time and cried out, "NNNNOOOOOO!!!"

I just lay there that morning trying hard to remember every detail about the dream. It was so vivid, and so real. I could not go back to sleep for a long time, and when I did, I barely slept an hour before I woke up, not cognizant of another dream during the last hour that my eyes were closed.

My Granny Gail was with me, that night—I just know it. She wanted me to finish the story. Looking back on my dream, my friend and her husband—both good people—represented the goodness in a grandmother that is still looking over me. The sand-like gravel driveway could be the driveway to the house that I knew as my home away from home when my grandmother was alive. The orange trees meant Florida, a place that she loved so dearly before her health kept her from visiting, and a place that played a big role in the writing of the first book. Not being able to give the car enough gas to get up that incline and not knowing what to do was definitely the decision I needed to make. I had to focus and set my mind to write this book. Having to pick the car up and point it in the right direction on that busy street meant that I was to go forward regardless of a busy life. My brother and his family buying a new home meant that life would go on, and my little sister, who has always had vivid dreams shrouded with family members who have passed, would take care of business in my absence. The old man in my dream was the same man that was there in the hospital in the days before Granny's death. No one at the hospital knew who he was, or had even seen him, but we all know he was there to escort Granny Gail from the burden of that failing body she no longer needed.

That dream epitomized everything my grandmother meant to her family and friends—charity, goodness, Godliness, home, closeness, and love—well, at least in the later years. My dream could be interpreted to mean anything, but I will always believe that the dream was my grandmother telling me to finish her story. All her life, she only needed to feel loved and wanted. With age comes wisdom, and as she aged, she worked hard to become a better grandmother than she ever was a mother. During much of her later life, we grandchildren were all she felt she had. Despite the bad decisions she made in her early years, Granny Gail tried as best she could to apologize to her daughters through her grandchildren. I want to make sure that the world knows she was incredibly humbled by her life choices and that she paid dearly through sacrifices that only a few people knew or will ever know.

I am very grateful to my mom and my aunt for allowing me to be involved with the first book. I admire them both, very much, because everything that happened to them over all those many years made them stronger women. *Lost in the Sins of Their Mother* helped my mother and my aunt to overcome much of the anger they harbored over the years, but now, my Granny Gail wants everyone to be able to love her the way her grandchildren loved —and still love—her. Her daughters had an opportunity to tell their side of the story, but now Gail wants to make sure that all is fair and she is able to tell her side.

Every generation passes down certain traits to the generation after. I am eternally grateful to my grandmother that I received the love in her heart, and one day, I hope to pass it on to someone else. Writing this book as if she were telling the story, hopefully, the readers will accept this as a possible explanation for some of the decisions she made through life. Maybe the reader can understand how she felt in the situations that formed the decisions through her life. I just want the reader to know that there are two sides to every tale.

# Chapter One
## *To My Daughters*

*"Amazing Grace, how sweet the sound, that saved a wretch like me. I once was lost, but now I am found, was blind but now I see."*

THAT TRULY WAS MY FAVORITE SONG. Hearing it gave me peace all my life, and I could never hear it enough. In my later years, over and over I would sing it to myself while I worked to gather vegetables from the fields, and it would continue in my head while I stood in the kitchen for hours and hours to get all those tomatoes and green beans and chow-chow into jars and freezer containers. I worked so hard, and I was so tired all the time, but I never stopped singing to myself. Looking back on my life, I can see how much joy and happiness people received from the blessings of my labors, and I can truly say that I was paid back tenfold for everything I did.

Even though I never got the chance to thank you both for such a wonderful day, I am telling you now that it meant more to me than any piece of chocolate or chicken biscuit anybody ever gave me. Dottie Bug's thoughts couldn't have been closer to the truth when she thought how much that day would have meant to me. You both knew how much I loved company, and never in my life have I felt more blessed than seeing everyone I loved come to visit me. Couldn't you just tell how proud I was? You both know how cold it can be in late February, so you know that beautiful day came straight from God, with the sun shining brightly across a sky that was bluer than any day God had created, warming the newly emerging grass that dotted the grounds around that beautiful old Victorian house on Jeff Davis Drive.

I know it was my fault, and my only wish would be that the people who loved me that much at my funeral could have shared it more when I was living. I wouldn't take a million dollars for that love, but I would gladly give it all for free. My wonderful daughters, I know now that I should have—and, in fact, could have—made different choices. Everyone always says that hindsight is 20/20. There is only one reason for that: it's true. However, my daughters, both of you have found that life brings on many choices. Sometimes decisions are made quickly, and the choices we make are made for a seemingly good reason at the time. If you will be honest about it, in your hearts, both of you know that you, too, have made some decisions you've had to stand by regardless of the outcome. Besides, you know from the stories I told you through the years, I never had many examples of good decision-making.

My daddy was a very domineering man and since my mama did what Daddy said, she seldom ever made any decisions. The decisions he made cost them all the money my mama's family had and they had to live with the outcome. I always felt a little begrudged as a child because we could have been so wealthy. The acres and acres of land that grew cotton would have provided enough money and power to have anything we'd want. Even during the Depression Years, we had everything: a fine home with servants to cook for us, a great future as leading members of society, and the potential to live like kings and queens. One of my favorite childhood memories was sitting on the old mammie's knee on that big front porch of the house my mama's family owned off Old National Highway in College Park while I listened to the stories she told us. I remember how big she was, able to hold two of us children on each knee, and we could never hear enough of the stories she told from the Bible. Oh, my! I can remember that like it was yesterday. I just can't remember her name. I must have gotten old, I guess.

Even though the price of cotton kept dropping, my daddy was determined that "Things'll get better! I ain't gonna sell cotton for no twenty cents a pound! Hell, NO!" Well, that decision cost Daddy everything Mama's family had worked so hard to achieve. He ended up losing our big old house and all that land, leaving just enough money to buy a few acres on the other side of the county. Instead of that big fine home my mama had known while growing up, they ended up raising eight kids in the four-room shack you girls remember them living in when you were children.

I suppose he must have learned from that mistake because, as well you know, in the years to follow, he turned that bad situation into a good enough living. By the time Mama had her eighth child and her female parts gave in to exhaustion that four-room house was chock-full and Mama and Daddy ended up with a lot of help in the tomato fields. Goodness, how I hated walking behind my mama watering tomato plants! But Mama always told me that "Anything worth having is worth working for. Besides, it ain't what you got, it's what you do with it." So, we all did our part, and kept on going. Before long, we forgot what it was like to not work, and finally came to know that our place in life was as a worker. The money my daddy made selling tomatoes at the Farmers Market kept us fed, but sometimes it felt to him like all he did was work to feed us, even though it always seemed to us that we did all the work!

Later on, when your daddy died, my life changed in ways that, hopefully, you will never know. Back then I never shared that period of time with you because I did love you. First you were too young. Then, before I knew it, you were gone. Afterwards, I was plain embarrassed and ashamed of it all. All I can tell you now, girls, is that the decisions I made—good and bad—well, I lived with the outcome a very long time. It tore me up inside and I thought about it on a daily basis. My life haunted the back of my thoughts every day, and into the nights. But never did those decisions come to the front of my thoughts more strongly than the day Dottie Bug made me realize that my time on earth might be ending soon.

I hope you both realize now how much pain I had gone through all my life. How many times I knew that God was punishing this old woman for what I had done in my younger years, and I prayed constantly for Him to forgive my errors. You have both read my journals, so you know how much ya'lls love meant to me. Spending so many years alone in the later part of my life, I had a lot of time to plead for forgiveness. God has forgiven me, and one day, I hope you will forgive me as well.

I married your step-daddy for a reason, too. Even if the reason was purely selfish. I had been through so much over the couple of years before we got together, and my life had been so full of turmoil. So many people had been mean to me since your daddy died and it had been so long since I felt wanted. You referred to my relationship with your step-daddy as "sins of the flesh." All I can say is that I was a healthy young woman, with the desires of a healthy young woman. With everything that was happening in my life at the time, I had ignored those desires for so long that I was very much in need of love. My need to feel loved again left me wanting nothing more than to feel wanted again. I didn't have anyone to help me make a better decision, so, I got caught up in another of life's choices. I knew that men wanted me, and sex made me feel better, and nothing made me feel needed more than that.

I will never say I made a bad choice, because Johnny and I really did enjoy each other's company before our health got bad. And, even though I missed the physical contact, we at least had someone to talk to, and, it did bring me Jenny and her children. Regardless of how life changed things over the years, I loved all my children and grandchildren. My little dahlins, I never realized how much partiality I showed her and her kids until you two wrote and told me how you felt. It may have seemed at times that I loved them more, but the truth is I always felt I had to compensate them in some way because you two were always much stronger than she was.

For that, my babies, I am truly sorry, but I cannot change the past. We can only make the best of life in the present and future. My time is past, but your times are now. Just remember what I told you, "Nothing ever goes over the dog's back that doesn't come up to its belly." You used to laugh at me, but now you both see that I am not just a crazy old woman. I have been a daughter, a sister, a wife, a mother, a grandmother, a great-grandmother, and a friend. I lived a long time and I saw a lot in that time. History repeats itself over and over again. I can only hope my mistakes will be a lesson for both of you and one day you can know what I know.

I am so proud of all my children and grandchildren. I love them all to pieces and I am so thankful to have left behind such a beautiful legacy. Please do what you can to keep them together as long as you can, because nothing in life is more precious than the gift of love. Anyone who ever loved and lost can understand how I felt over the last few years of my life. It's hell to get old, but it doesn't have to be lonely. I hope that when you look back over your life, you can see where you've been, and be proud of what you've done. Pride is a wonderful thing, but pride can also hinder life's progress. Keep your faith in God, and keep your faith in yourself. Prove your love to yourself, and it will reflect in your love to others.

Even though my story will be told after the fact, hopefully, it will give a different view of my decisions for you to think about. Besides, it *could* be closer to true than anyone will be able to dispute. Keith always did look at the bright side so I hope you will love me even more when this book is finished.

Patti Cake, do you remember when I kept telling you I had something to tell you, but I never thought it was the right time? You and Dottie Bug had some learning to do—some growing up in your own lives. When you two were living through the last few weeks of my life, you discovered more about me than you ever knew before. The facts you discovered weren't dormant; they were hidden by me and the few others that knew them. What you and Dottie Bug found out was traumatic and it confused you, but at least you know more of the truth, and I hope you can both understand why I kept so much from you, and you will forgive me along the way.

Both of you have things in your life you want to keep private, so you have to know that my past was a real embarrassment to my proud daddy and mama, and no one ever wanted to talk about it. I would have loved to have shared more of my life with you, but you had problems of your own. Quite honestly, I had hidden so much for so long that I feared you might not understand. Since my death, I have been very close to you both, and both of you have felt my presence. I will always be there with you, and I will always love you more than life itself. But it is time you hear the story from a different perspective—mine. All I ever had in life was love; all I wanted in life was to be needed; and everything I did in life was because of my need for love.

*Now, Patti Cake and Dottie Bug, I got sumthin' to tell you, and now is the right time.*

## Chapter Two
### *My First Love*

YES, TIMES *WERE* HARD FOR MY mama and daddy, especially my mama, who felt like a baby machine for the longest time. Eight kids were a lot to handle—and yes, Dottie Bug, giving birth in those days was more than any woman should have to bear. My mama's female parts were so worn out that she was actually glad it was over. There wasn't much time for recovery after each birth and if not for the goodness of other women folk to help her out during the baby years, she, too, could have given out and given up. Nonetheless, true grit was always my mother's best asset. Both of you get that from her, and both of you should be proud she was as strong as she was. She taught us all to respect God and each other, and since she taught us straight out of the Bible, we all knew what prayer was. Even with such a big family, God was always good to us.

As children, we yearned to get away from the hard lives we had; but, as we looked back later in life, we were all so very thankful we had lived when we did. When Mama and Daddy lost that big old house and we moved to that little shack in the red dirt fields of Clayton County, that respect for God was all they had. Every day we would get up to the sounds of our daddy and mama getting the day going. We didn't have much to eat according to today's standards, but we all got fed, and the small portions of food never hurt us. Sure, we were lanky and lean, but we all turned out healthy.

With only one good set of clothes to wear, we had to make sure to take care of them, because when we outgrew them, we had to pass it on to the next youngin'. That wasn't so bad for the oldest, because they always got new clothes, but to the younger ones, it usually caused a stir of cries that Mama would have to quiet. Usually she made it OK by making us a batch of teacakes, like the ones I used to make for you two girls. Daddy was always tight with money, and sometimes we felt like he was trying to take it with him to the grave. We always wondered why he was like that, and I guess no one will ever know.

Children today have no idea what it's like to work hard. Try getting one of today's children to walk for miles with a bucket, dipping a small tin cup full of water at the base of a thousand little tomato plants as each is put into the ground and covered up to the first two leaves, just to make sure it would get a good root system started. I know I couldn't have carried anything any bigger, but my, oh, my, how I thought that bucket was too small! It was almost as big as me, and when it was full, it probably weighed more than I did. Walking back to the watering well what seemed like a thousand times a day, I grew to hate tomatoes. In my later years, I often wondered if my mama ever hated those fields as much as I did when I was young. If she did, she never let on. She just kept on planting.

As those little plants grew and flowered, then developed tiny tomatoes, we would have to walk those fields all over again, picking off the bad ones, picking off tomato worms, and making sure they had enough water. Once they matured, and started ripening again we would have to walk those God-awful miles of row after row of tomatoes as we picked hundreds and hundreds of those red balls of juice each day. Sometimes, we would be so tired we would get giggly. The more we giggled and laughed, the heavier those baskets got to us and we would usually get scolded by Mama or Daddy. Heck, we were just kids! But we had our job to do, and periodically throwing one or two tomatoes at each other, or one of the crows waiting for us to leave so they could eat was all the entertainment we could find.

Year after year, we did that, until we were old enough to go to school. Then we only had to work that hard in the afternoons. Only it was worse then, because we had friends we would rather spend time with. After school, all the way until sundown; we would work until sundown and it was time to eat. Mama would leave the fields earlier than we did to fix dinner, and even though we wanted to leave right behind her, Daddy would make us stay until he was ready to go. That last row every afternoon was the longest one of the day, so you can imagine that quite a few bugs might have been given another day to eat at what I started calling "the tomato plant buffet."

After we ate, we girls would help Mama clean up the dishes and we would all have to do our homework. There was no electricity at our house. Heck, it was a long way to what people these days call civilization. It could take a good part of the day just to go to town, and that was something we kids never got to do, anyway. Once the sun went down, it was dark in the house so we had to do our homework by lamplight, or by the light coming from the stove. It is no wonder why all of us needed glasses over the years.

Soon, working the fields and then carrying the crates of tomatoes to the Farmers Market was more than Daddy could do with the limited help he had available, so Daddy decided that since a woman didn't need much of an education, I should stay out of school and help Mama with the workload. To him, after all, a woman's place was in the home. Well, I have to admit, I did enjoy not going to school every day, but life couldn't have been any more miserable to me than while I was walking those God-awful tomato fields all day.

I was just about 12 years old when I started feeling as though I was missing something and I suddenly developed a hankering for boys. Whenever I saw a good-looking boy about my age, I went crazy. Emotions stirred in the pit of my soul that would almost bring me to my knees. I know you both know how I felt. After all, you're both women now, and you've both felt the tingly feeling that only a man can bring on. OK, I know! You get embarrassed hearing that kind of talk from your ole' mother, but you both know what I mean. Anyway, that's another story for another chapter. Besides, there was a different, much stronger, love calling for me about that same time. I kept hearing it. When I heard it, my feet moved back and forth as though I had been rehearsing for it all my life. I found that I loved music and I couldn't hear it often enough.

As you know, your Uncle Calvin—we always called him Brother—was quite a bit older than me. It was 1935 and Brother had already joined the Navy. Whenever he would come home on a furlough, sometimes he would borrow Daddy's truck and go to the honky-tonk to have a drink and visit with some of his old friends. He would be out in the fields the next day singing to himself, or humming a new song he'd heard the night before and I would to listen to him as he sang those songs over, and over. He didn't have much of a singing voice, but he would give it his all, and just the melody would get my feet to tapping back and forth. I would memorize the tune and I would just imagine hearing it over a speakerphone with real music. Brother would whistle tunes like "Can the Circle Be Unbroken" by the Carter Family; or he would sing "The Sunny Side of Life" by the Blue Sky Boys. I learned every word he sang, and he would smile real big at me as I sang along with him, all the while dreaming about getting away from the house and going to hear them for myself.

For the next few months as I walked that million miles of red dirt, watering plants, picking them damned bugs off them, and picking tomatoes as they got ripe enough, over and over again I pretended I was dancing at the honky-tonk, or standing in front of a bunch of good-looking men while I performed a song or two. Every day that passed, I dreamed about it, and every time Brother came home from there, I would add another song to my list of favorites. The four rooms with all those kids piled together like a jar of pickled eggs got me feeling cramped for the last time. When the walls literally felt like they were squeezing the breath out of me, I decided it was time, and I started devising a plan to sneak away.

I'd been watching that back door for over a week. I listened close as that heavy door opened and closed and soon I knew just when the old skeleton key doorknob clicked, and exactly at what point that heavy door started to squeak when it opened. I opened and closed that old farmhouse door more than a hundred times until I finally figured it out. If I lifted up on it just as it left the doorframe, I could avoid that squeak. I even figured out how to push in on the door before I turned the doorknob so it didn't click very loud. Then, one evening, I waited until Mama and Daddy, and the other kids, had gone to bed and I felt like most of them had gone to sleep. Then I waited until Daddy started snoring. I knew that, as loud as he snored, only a freight train running through the house would wake him up. When I eased out of bed, I heard Little Stan ask me where I was going. I told him I was going to the outhouse and that he should go on to sleep. *What a sweet kid*, I thought, as I leaned over, kissed him good night, and told him I loved him. As he rolled over and closed his eyes again, I couldn't help but feel a little partial to him.

I was scared to death about what I was fixing to do, but I had made up my mind that I wanted to do this, and nothing was going to stand in my way. As soon as I felt comfortable enough, with my throat dry and my heart pounding in my chest so hard I thought it would bust open the blouse I had put on, I tiptoed through the house. I pushed on the door so the lock wouldn't click very loud, turned the knob real slow, making sure to lift up on the door at the very spot the creak started, then, I slipped outside. I gently closed the door behind me, carefully lifting up again at just the right time, and I slowly let go of the old doorknob so the door closed real secure and I let go. I stood there for what seemed like hours, nervous and feeling like I could throw up, listening for sounds of anyone stirring inside the house; not one sound. I turned to walk down the steps, and seemed to skip most of them as I ran on the tips of my toes down the driveway into the pitch-black night. The closer I got to the road, the faster I ran. The farther I got from the house, the bigger the grin on my face grew. I was on my way to answer a calling!

    I guess it was about 10:00 in the evening. It was quite a ways down to the honky-tonk that Brother had bragged about, so I figured I had a while to hike. It turned out that Lady Luck was with me that night. I got to the edge of Riverdale Road at just the right time because a man about my daddy's age in an old Ford pickup truck happened to be driving by on his way into town. He must have thought I was older than I was which, in the end, turned out to be in my favor. He said his wife was "in the family way" and she couldn't travel with him that night so he would appreciate the conversation to help him stay awake. He told me he was on his way to Riverdale to pick up her family from the train bringing them from Birmingham and he asked me where I was going so late at night. I remembered how my mama always told me that lying is a sin and I was afraid to burn in the after life. I acted like I didn't hear him the first time and shyly said, "Huh?" That bought me a couple of extra seconds to think.

    My young mind was telling me that this man was probably a friend of my daddy's or something and if he knew I was only thirteen years old and on my way to a honky-tonk, he might turn around and take me home. So I told him I was headed into town to meet my brother. After all, that wasn't a complete lie. If Brother was there, I would see him. Besides, I would need a ride home and riding in the truck with Brother was sure better than hitching a ride or walking. I kept quiet about my real intentions, and I was glad that he didn't ask many more questions. As he drove nearer to town, I told him I had to pee and asked him to stop so I could get out because I could walk the rest of the way. I thanked him, opened the door, and got out of his old Ford truck. I had to look like I was going over into the brush, but as soon as he drove off I was high-tailing my watusie down the road to the honky-tonk. I could already hear the music and the laughing and my feet were twitching like there was no tomorrow.

When I got to the plain red dirt parking lot, I was so nervous I felt like throwing up again. There were several cars parked out front and several more parked out to the side. A couple of guys were leaning against one of the cars, a convertible with the top down and it was so beautiful that I swore to myself that some day I would own me one of them. I took in every sight my eyes could take in, absorbing every sound and every smell, and I felt that energy all the way to my soul. Mostly, I felt it in my toes. All ten of the long, skinny toes at the end of my thirteen-year-old feet had a mind of their own and they were coordinating their energies like they already knew what to do. The two men leaning on the convertible had a brown paper bag they were passing back and forth and they each took turns sipping from the bottle inside.

As I got closer to them, one of them nudged the other one and pointed over at me with his thumb. They both whistled at me and then chuckled. At first, I felt a bit embarrassed, but I just held my head up like I was the Queen Mary herself. I ran my finger down the length of the car they were leaning on and swayed my shoulders back and forth with a coy little grin. As I walked by them, they elbowed each other again, and laughed, then continued to pass the bottle back and forth. From the corner of my eye, I made sure I was past them before I let go of the huge grin of a 13-year-old girl. In my mind, I was already a hit, and I had made it past my first test. Now, I just had to get through the front door.

The old building wasn't much to look at, but it served its purpose and I didn't care. I just wanted to hear the music and dance. I walked up to the bright red door and I reached for the handle. My arm was about halfway there when suddenly I froze. Girls, you don't know how scared your mama was at that moment. All of a sudden, my mind conjured up images of me walking in the room and everyone pointing at me. I imagined all of them yelling at me and telling me I was too young to be there.

I imagined the truant officer grabbing me and taking me home to my daddy. My throat was dry again, as I swallowed hard. *OK, girl! Get it together! You made it this far, might as well go on in!*

I grabbed that door handle like it was an old axe handle and pulled on it hard. I had butterflies in my stomach, and I was still feeling like I wanted to throw up. But as soon as I opened that door, the smell of cigarette smoke, whiskey, and sweat, mixed with the energy flowing inside that honky-tonk eased everything I was feeling. Everything, that is, but that calling I came to answer. The music was louder than I had ever imagined it could be, and I was immediately drawn into a world I just knew was going to be my home away from home! Can you picture it? This tall, skinny, long-legged girl, with wavy, strawberry-blond hair, skin darkened from being outside all the time, only 13 years old and walking into a honky-tonk?

My daddy always told me I would never have a problem finding a man. I suppose that was his way of telling me I was pretty. I would soon find out if he was telling the truth, or not! As I stepped into the bar, all the guys, even the ones with other women, glanced over at me, then did a double take, almost staring at me. They all got big smiles on their face. A few of the women got a bit perturbed, and one of the women grabbed the collar of the shirt her man was wearing, jerking his face back around to face her. I must be pretty, after all!

What butterflies? I held my head up, with that same coy little grin I had earlier, and I forgot all about my butterflies. I tried not to look like a child as I walked around the room, taking in all the sights and sounds. There wasn't much to the place, mostly a few tables along the walls, a wooden table in one corner where a man was selling beer and what I guessed was whiskey. In the center of the large open building, there were men and women dancing in the middle of a large wooden floor. The huge jukebox, a shiny brand-new Wurlitzer, stood in the corner of the room and I slowly made my way over to it. I read to myself all the songs that were in the machine, and even though I only knew a few of them, I was looking forward to hearing all of them. Only thing was, I hadn't brought any money with me. I hadn't thought about that part of my journey, but at least I was there. I had made it this far, and so far, I had not had any problems. I was swaying back and forth to the music, bent over slightly to read the song titles, when I heard a voice over my shoulder. It scared the devil out of me and I knew immediately that I had been caught! It was Brother! He had seen me come in the bar, and had followed me around the room.

"What the HELL are you doin' in here?" he yelled. "How did you get here? Come on, I'm taking you home and Daddy's gonna tan your hide!"

I was panic-stricken, but I was determined I wasn't going home yet. He had me by the arm and was squeezing hard. I twisted my body several times before I got loose from him and looked at him with a grin only a sister can give a brother.

"Now, Brother, come on," I said. "Won't you please let me stay for just one dance? I won't tell Mama and Daddy you let me do it. PLEASE? I just want to hear one song. I love you." I was sure he couldn't say no to that and I was right.

"Well, you can stay for one song, but that's it! I mean it! We're both gonna get a whoopin' if anyone finds out!"

So far, I had jumped every hurdle I came to, and I felt like I had gone to Heaven. I ended up dancing alone for the first dance, but soon, my dance card was full. I had men lined up waiting for their turn with the little lady who loved to dance! Not one of them realized how young I was. I don't guess it mattered. I was fun to dance with, even if I did make up the moves as I went along. All of a sudden, the music stopped. I looked around and noticed most of the women gathering in the middle of the floor. The guys started clapping, and yelling and whistling as they moved the tables and chairs to the wall. When that big ole' Wurlitzer started back up and Benny Goodman, the new "King of Swing" came blaring from the speakers, I just stood and watched. All at one time, the women started a dance one of the guys said was the Charleston. I watched for a second or two, but I just had to get out there and join. Soon I had found my favorite dance! I got so good at it that no one could keep up with me. I guess Brother had found something else to think about because he wasn't lurking over me anymore. I looked around for him, but didn't put much effort into finding him. I was really enjoying myself but around the fourth dance, I was getting thirsty.

All they had to drink there was whiskey and beer. Everyone was drinking it, and they all seemed to be having a good time. I thought about it for a minute and worked up enough nerve to ask the man behind the wooden table if I could taste one. He handed me a little brown bottle and asked me for my money. I was horrified, and, judging from his chuckle, it must have showed. He saw the expression on my face, smiled real big and said, "Never mind, young lady! You've been the entertainment tonight. This one's on the house."

"Thank you, kindly!" I said, hoping I didn't sound too much like a child. I smiled the same coy little grin I'd been practicing on every other man that night. I held the bottle in my hand for a second or two, trying to get up the nerve to drink it.

There were some people standing behind me waiting to get a drink and one of the girls with them said, "You gonna stand there all night? We want something to drink! Get a move on!"

As I turned to see who it was, I saw the same woman who had grabbed her man's shirt collar earlier. I threw my shoulders back, threw her a dirty look, cocked my head to one side and smugly walked right by her. I was sure getting used to being there. I knew exactly why Brother liked coming here and I couldn't wait to get back. I still had that little brown bottle in my hand as I walked around the room again and I ended up standing next to the dance floor. I noticed that Brother was busy talking with a number of people and he seemed to have forgotten all about me. *Finally*, I thought. I looked down at that drink. I sure was thirsty. I brought the drink to my mouth, opened my pretty little lips, and anxiously waited for the taste of my first alcoholic beverage. I took a little sip. *OOOHHH*, it was so good! It was cold, and it was smooth as the ice cream Mama made us in the summer! I put the bottle to my lips again; only this time, I drank it like it was water.

"Whoah, girl! They're still making it!"

It startled me, and I almost spit out what was in my mouth already. I turned to see a guy, obviously a few years older than me, standing there holding a bottle of his own. He was great looking, with his dark wavy hair, and the deepest brown eyes I had ever seen on anyone. His skin was darker than mine with an olive color to it and he had a great smile. He was wearing a plain white tee shirt and pair of jeans. It seemed to be what almost every one of the men were wearing, even some of the women; although a couple of the women wore dresses, and a couple of the guys wore overalls, Brother being one of them. He didn't seem to notice how young I was, and soon, I forgot that I was even worried about anyone finding out. We chatted for a few minutes and I found out he usually met some friends here, but that night he just came to dance.

He had been watching me all night and was hoping to get to dance with me. We were out on the floor before he even finished asking, and soon we were sweating up a storm. He offered to buy me a drink, and, *as any Southern lady should do*, I politely obliged his request. After all, it sure was good! But I wanted to taste that whiskey everyone seemed to be enjoying! I didn't have the same nervous feeling as with the beer I had earlier as I brought the drink straight to my lips. I figured it was going to taste smooth as ice cream like before, so I just tossed my head back and swallowed it in one gulp. No sooner had I swallowed it, I felt my throat burn like a bad case of strep throat and I felt a fire in my stomach that caught me off-guard and took my breath away! The good-looking stranger laughed at me, asking if that was my first taste of whiskey. Still trying to hide my age, I stood up straight and with as much dignity as I could muster, I told him, "No." I swallowed again. "No, I just swallowed it wrong."

The burning stopped, and I realized that it wasn't bad. In fact, I wanted another one. He smiled and got me another, and then another. Soon, with one beer and three shots of whiskey in my young belly, I was feeling good. So good, in fact, that I was dancing all over the place. I ended up getting on top of one of the tables while the men cheered me on. I was doing the Charleston, which, like I said, had become my favorite dance with all my heart. It was so hot in there. I was sweaty, and my head was swimming, but I wasn't about to stop. Instead, I just decided to take off my blouse. Shoot, I didn't care, and the cheering crowd didn't seem to mind either.

Brother heard the cheering getting louder. He realized he had lost track of me, and figured he might need to make sure I was OK. He heard all the commotion and pushed his way through 'til he got to the front of the crowd. Brother couldn't believe his eyes! He tried to grab me off the table, but the men watching kept pulling him away.

"GAIL! GAIL! GET OFF THERE! GET OFF THERE RIGHT NOW! GOSH DANGIT! GET OFF THAT TABLE! I CAN'T BELIEVE YOU!"

Brother quickly realized that crowd wasn't going to let him stop me from dancing on the table with my bra on and he stood there wondering what to do. He knew already he was going to be in trouble when he told Daddy he didn't take me home when I snuck out, but if anything happened to me, that trouble was going to be worse. He figured he would rather be in trouble for something he'd done instead of something he hadn't done, so he tried one more time to get me off the table.

Mad and shaking his head, he ran out that bright red door, got into that old pickup truck and drove home fast as he could to tell Daddy. Brother pulled in the yard in a hurry, ran up the stairs and pushed open the back door I left unlocked. He ran into the house shouting, "DADDY! DADDY! You got to come get Gail! She's down at the honky-tonk dancing on the tables with nuthin' but her panties and brassier on! Hurry! Before she gets into more trouble!"

By the time Daddy and Brother came into the honky-tonk, I had finished my dance. Actually, I fell off the table. Oh, I didn't hurt myself, but I was sure tired. Before I realized what had happened, I felt the strongest pair of arms lift me up and sit me on the chair next to the table. It was the same good-looking stranger who had bought me my first drink. I never did get his name, but he stood by me and took care of me until my daddy got there. I kept looking at him as the drinks wore off and I could see clearer. He was definitely a few years older than me, and in fact, it seemed like he was not much younger than my daddy. But he was kind and treated me with dignity and I couldn't help but feel like I knew him from somewhere. Anyways, where would a 13-year-old girl have met a man like him? I just chocked it up to "one of those things" and forgot about it. Besides, Brother and Daddy were driving up, and Daddy was madder than a hornet. He didn't speak, he just told Brother to put me in the truck. Daddy went up to the man, spoke for a minute or two, and I saw them shaking hands as if they knew each other. I decided that I must have seen him somewhere around my daddy's tomato business. Yeah, that must be it. Anyway, the ride home was short, because I fell asleep before we left that dirt parking lot.

That, my daughters, is the story of dancing, my first love.

# Chapter Three
## *Maxwell Jackson*

WHEN I GOT HOME, BROTHER CARRIED me into the house and flopped me down on the settee, covered me up with the old blanket Mama had lying across the red chair my daddy used to sit on, the same one ya'll remember; that red one the snuff bucket sat beside. Anyway, the next morning, when I woke up, Ellie and Stan were sitting on the floor in front of me, watching like I was going to do tricks or something. My eyes opened a little and the light was burning a hole into the back of my head.

"Mama! Gail's done woke up!" Ellie yelled out to Mama in the kitchen, sounding like she screamed right into my ear as loud as she could. I swung out at her but only managed to fall off the edge of the settee, my fall seeming to entertain both of them greatly.

"Well, it's about time you decided to join us, young lady. Your breakfast is on a plate by the stove. Eat and change your clothes. We got work to do."

That was all my mama said. I think the lack of words was more hurtful to me than if she had asked me to go out and pick a hickory stick so she could stripe my legs good. I went over to the old wood-burning stove and found the plate of food she left for me, but couldn't bring myself to eat anything. I had a horrible taste in my mouth, worse than green persimmons in March. Ellie had already gone outside and was helping Mama draw some water in buckets. Stan was still in the kitchen with me, at the little table, staring at me with my head propped on my folded arm.

"Where'd you go last night, sister? They was whisperin' kind a low, but I heard 'em talkin' 'bout you today. They was real mad. Deddy's been gone since early today and he told Mama he might be late comin' home."

I tried to think about last night, but all I could remember was that nice-looking guy buying me that drink that burned like a haystack soaked in kerosene. God! *What DID I do last night?*

I looked around for Brother, but he had already gone out to the fields to plow for Daddy. I ate as much as I could, and put what I didn't want back on the stove. Mama always said, "Waste not, want not." So I put a napkin over the buttered biscuit and slice of ham that was left. I guess that is where I got the habit of putting my leftover biscuits in the oven so ya'll could have one when you came over. Well, I looked around under piles of clothes until I found my dungarees. I changed my blouse, putting on my red and white checked shirt, put on my old hat, and walked out the back door to where my chores waited. I couldn't help but smile as I almost unconsciously opened that door real slow, lifting it up at just the right time, so as to avoid that squeak. As I walked down those steps, memories of the night before came flooding into my mind. Suddenly, I almost didn't mind having to lift those buckets of water. I said, *ALMOST.*

I still hated it, but my mind had some wonderful thoughts, and I had brand-new songs in my head, and music to go along with them this time! I almost tripped walking towards the well as my feet started reliving the night before. Well, that, and my ankle kind of hurt from the fall I took off that table. It was a long time that day before my mama ever spoke to me. We were cleaning up after our long walks through the tomato plant buffet when she spoke up.

"You know your daddy was real mad, don't ya? He went off to speak to that man you was dancing with last night. Gail, you ain't all grown up yet. Don't let your eyes get bigger 'n your stomach. Bein' grown ain't all fun and games and you got a powerful lot of learnin' to do. I hope that feeling you had this mornin' lingers, so you can remember it. You don't need be startin' no bad habits. I taught you better than that."

That was all she said the rest of the day. It was a long time before Daddy came home and he wouldn't even look at me. He didn't have to. The words from my mama's mouth had been enough to make me wish I hadn't gone. Well, almost. At least for a few days 'til I started having that urge again.

Over the next few weeks, I was good as gold. I had to be, because Brother was watching me like a hawk. The summer was coming to a close, and we found ourselves with a little more time to play. With less to do in the fields, Daddy started going on trips, sometimes staying gone for days. We never knew, at the time, where he went, but years later, when I found out where he was disappearing to, it didn't surprise me much. Well, there again, another story for another chapter. I had figured out how long Daddy would be gone after he left and I took full advantage of those nights. I would slip out after I figured everyone was asleep and head back to the honky-tonk to listen and dance just long enough to quench that thirst I had.

When I was seven years old and we lived in that big old house, one of Daddy's field helpers taught me how to roll cigarettes. I used to sneak some out of Daddy's little, silver Prince Albert tobacco can he thought was hidden. That field hand taught me how to roll a perfectly round cigarette and even how to smoke it and without choking. Now, not so many years later, there I was, a honky-tonk regular, smoking, drinking and dancing my legs off. For the next few months, Mama and Daddy tried their best to keep me tamed, always threatening to send me to a reformatory school for girls. Thankfully, he never did. I guess he finally just gave up on me. Figuring as long as I was doing my share of the work, he would just have to overlook me. Somehow I didn't mind the work anymore, and my happy thoughts helped me through the day's labors.

It was almost time for Brother to head back to the Navy. They had let him out long enough to help on the farm, but since the summer was almost over, his furlough was ending. He asked Daddy if it would be OK for one of his Navy buddies to come visit for a few days before they headed back. Brother explained that his family owned a bunch of land in Clayton County and he had been spending his furlough helping his grandmother run her company. They were going to take the train back to the base together, but his friend wanted to meet the family before they left. Daddy said it was OK, so Brother headed out in the truck to pick him up. He was only going to spend a couple of weeks with us, but Daddy never knew how those couple of weeks were going to change all our lives.

It was late on Friday when Brother brought him to the house. They drove up to the old farmhouse, and when the truck stopped, it must have been a sight to Brother's friend, because it looked like a schoolyard when we seven kids, and Mama and Daddy came walking to the truck, seemingly from everywhere. We didn't get much company around there, especially overnight guests. As soon as the door opened and I saw the beautiful man who got out of the passenger side door, my mind went to racing and I thought every nerve in my body was going to break open as every ounce of blood left my head. Every ounce of adrenaline in my body started rushing around as if the governor just pulled up out front and I hadn't cleaned the house yet. His name was Maxwell Jackson and he was the most handsome man I had ever seen! Even though I was taller than most girls my age, he was still much taller than me, and so muscular! His dark eyes sparkled like huge black diamonds under his deep tanned skin and beautiful, dark, naturally curly hair. I couldn't help but wonder if he was Italian. He shook everyone's hand, and gave Mama the handful of flowers he had picked in his grandmother's garden before they left. Each of the kids giggled as he said hello to him. Then he came to say hello to me.

I had positioned myself at the end of the bunch because my hormones were already busy devising a plan to flirt with him. When he got to me, he asked, "And who might you be, pretty lady?"

"How do you do? My name is Gail."

I curtsied, giving him the same coy little grin I had practiced so many times. I offered him my hand as I rose from my curtsy and he gently held my fingers to his lips as he kissed my long fingertips. I never lost eye contact with him, nor did he lose any with me. His large perfectly white teeth were shining as he smiled. I could tell that his hormones were gathering up for a run through the fields as well.

Max and I both found our affection for each other growing from the very day he arrived and the next two weeks went by too fast for our liking. Max wanted me just as much as I wanted him, and nothing would do except for us to sneak off somewhere to be alone for even a minute. A couple of days before he and Brother were supposed to leave, Max and I snuck off into the woods behind the house and he asked me to marry him and be his wife. I guess no one ever told him how old I was, and I certainly wasn't going to either. It didn't matter to me that he was older, and I never did look like a child. Besides, I had already been playing the role of a grown-up, hadn't I? I could dance, and drink, and smoke, and all the other men in town liked me, didn't they? I wanted to be Mrs. Maxwell Jackson, and no one, not even my daddy, was going to stop me. I don't know what kind of women he was used to meeting, but I was really surprised that he hadn't already grabbed him up. Surprised, but happy it hadn't happened yet. We both knew we had met our soul mates. We didn't want to get married in Clayton County because we were afraid someone would be able to stop us, so we decided to go over to the next county. In the middle of the night, we stole Daddy's truck, and, in the cloak of darkness, headed off to get married, never dreaming it would be as short as it was.

The next morning, when Mama, Daddy and all my brothers and sisters found out I was gone, it didn't surprise them much, because they were used to me sneaking off at night. They just figured I had finally forgotten about time, or maybe had a hard time getting a ride back home from the honky-tonk. But a few minutes later when they realized that Max was also missing, along with the truck, Daddy started yelling, "What's that girl done gone and gotten into now?"

"Now, Lloyd, don't go making assumptions, I'm sure there is a good reason why they gone off together."

Mama came to my defense, but neither of them would have ever considered what they were about to find out. Max and I drove up a little after the lunch was being cleaned up. I was so happy, but, of course, Max was very nervous because he'd never done anything like that before. Daddy heard us coming up the driveway and met Max at the door of the truck before Max could even open it.

"Boy, you got a lot of explainin' to do. Where the HELL you been with my girl and my truck? SPEAK, BOY!"

Max was nervous as a long-tailed cat in a rocking chair tournament, as he described to my daddy how much he loved me and that he knew they should have talked before we eloped.

"But," he explained, "sir, I have never met anyone like your daughter. I was madly in love with her since the second I saw her two weeks ago. I know it was impolite, but I will take care to provide the very best for her. We were meant to be together, sir, and I wanted to make sure she was mine before I headed back to the base."

Mama took me by the arm and led me into the house, telling the other kids there was work to be done while the grown folks talked.

*Hmmm*, I thought, *grown folks*. Yeah, that was me. "Grown folks." My mama made me feel ten feet tall just then, but it didn't last long. Once we got inside, she scolded me bad with the facts of life. She said if I was going to act like a grown-up woman, I needed to know what a grown-up woman had to do. She told me, for the first time, about the birds and the bees. Goodness, to hear her talk, being with a man was a nasty act that had to be done just to make sure you had kids to help out around the house. Nothing she told me mentioned anything about love, affection, foreplay, or satisfaction that can come out of two people making love. Instead, she described how a man will crawl up on you whenever he wanted to, do his business, and then go to sleep. I didn't even know what kind of questions to ask her. I had feelings inside me that I wondered about, like boys, monthly cycles, if it ever felt good to the woman, or even to the man. She got irritated with my questions, and soon she changed the subject.

Afterwards, Mama and Daddy sat us down and asked us where we were gonna stay. Daddy said there just wasn't anymore room in the house. "And besides," Daddy said, "ain't no house big enough for two families."

Max agreed that we would find a place to stay until he left in a few days, so Brother took us to town to find a room. He and Max barely spoke on the way, because Brother was so upset and disappointed that his friend would do this. Brother is actually the one that finally broke the ice.

"I can't believe you would do this. You know, don't ya, that she is only 13?" Now, he did it! My heart sank as I felt Max's eyes cut over to me, sitting in the middle of these two men having what I thought was a petty tiff. I could have crawled under the floorboard, as I looked at Max, gleaming at me with those big, black diamonds of his. I wondered what was going on between his ears, and I grabbed his left knee and squeezed it 'til he wrapped his left arm around me and hugged me close.

"I can't help it, Cal. I love this girl with all my heart and I intend on being the best husband ever known."

I have never in my life felt that deep of a love. Not even later on with ya'lls daddy. Max turned out to be the best thing that ever happened to me. I was prepared to fight for him and nothing was going to stand in my way of being happy.

Brother pulled over near the middle of town. He and Max

barely said good-bye to each other as Brother walked off towards the drugstore for some cornmeal and butter for Mama. Max and I grabbed the sack full of my clothes and his duffle bag and walked toward the hotel. I suddenly became aware of people staring at us. I grabbed Max by the hand as I began to see them looking at us and whispering something to each other. "Never mind them, Gail, honey. They're just jealous. It's been so long since they seen anyone in love, they just got to talk about it."

As we entered the hotel lobby, well, I call it a lobby, it was barely a furnished room, with only a chair and a table in it just big enough for someone to sit at while they filled out their registration card. There was a half wall across from the entrance where a woman about my mama's age stood. She looked me up and down, then looked over at Max.

"Can I help you?" she asked with a smirk on her face. After that first look at me, she never looked at me again.

"My bride and I want to get a room for the next two days before I head out to the Navy base."

"Certainly," she said coldly.

She told him how much the room would be and, as he paid her, she threw a key down on the countertop, pointing to a set of steps that led to a dimly lit hallway upstairs. As we walked up the creaky stairs, I got nervous. My mama had me really worried about my duties as a woman. In all my nights at the honky-tonk, and all the flirting I did with men, I had never taken them up on their advances, always able to smile my way out of things and maintain my virginity. Until now, that is. Max opened the door leading into a single room. There was only a bed, a little dresser and a sink basin like Mama and Daddy had in their room. Max held my hand with that same gentle touch, and led me into the room, closing the door behind us, separating us from the rest of the world and the last glimpse of my childhood. As I went over and sat on the corner of the bed, if ever there was a time that I felt like a child, that very moment, on the very brink of becoming a woman, was that time.

Max, suddenly aware of my age, figured I must be nervous.

Instead of immediately doing what a newlywed couple would do on their honeymoon, he just sat on the bed next to me, wrapped his right arm around me, his left hand gently cupping my chin, and pulled my head onto his shoulder. I was frozen. My mama's voice kept ringing in my ears. I began to cry, and soon I was blubbering into his shoulder everything Mama said about the birds and the bees. After a few minutes, I noticed that Max was laughing. I sat up straight, pissed off because he was laughing.

"Just what are you laughin' at, Maxwell Jackson? It's not funny! Sure, you have nothing to be scared about. 'Doing it' is all good for you. I am scared it's gonna hurt. My mama wouldn't tell me a story!"

Max did his best to hold back his laughing as he put both his hands on my face and pulled me into him, gently kissing me on the lips as he said, "There. Did that hurt?"

I couldn't tell a lie, it actually felt good. He kissed me again.

Again he asked, "Did that?"

"Well," I said shyly, "no."

Max took me into his arms and gave me a huge, deep, tongue-twisting kiss that left me speechless.

"How was that?" he asked me softly.

By now all those hormones that had been racing inside me focused on one area in particular. As if being instructed to do so, I leaned into him, folding my arms around him like he was my favorite teddy bear, and responded with a kiss of my own. It was the most sensitive experience I ever had since. It was going to be my first time, and Max was making sure it was a memorable experience. I didn't even notice as he unbuttoned the blouse I was wearing. I did, however, notice when he stood up and took off his shirt. If I had any hesitations before then, they went out the badly-in-need-of-cleaning window overlooking the street below. He was so sweet as he stood me up, pulled back the cheap bedcovers on what was to be the chariot to my womanhood, and gently laid me down. He slowly lay beside me, pushing his arm under me like a pillow, and leaned into me, gently kissing my face, neck and shoulders. The rest of the evening was spent in that little hotel room at the top of those creaky stairs, overlooking the street. It was magic.

The next day, I woke up a woman. Max, the man I loved more than life itself, was already getting dressed when I woke up. I was surprised to see him getting ready to walk out the door, wondering if he was going to tell me where he was going.

"Good morning, sunshine," he said with a gentle kiss on my cheek.

"Maxwell, where you goin' so early?"

"Gail, I love you, you know that? Well, I have to visit my family and tell them how much I love you, and tell them I got married yesterday."

I was still half asleep as the child inside me asked, "Can't I come with you?"

He finished tying his shoe and reached into his pocket. "I'll be back shortly. Here is a couple of dollars. Get one of the buggies to carry you back to your mama's house, and I'll come back there to get you." I was heartbroken that the night was over, but I knew he had to tell his folks, so I kissed him as he walked out the door. I got up, dressed, and walked down those creaky stairs past the lady at the desk. She looked over her glasses at me but never spoke a word.

The events of last night had left me with terrible hunger pains, so I decided to take the money Max gave me and buy something to eat at the little restaurant across the street. I walked in, and felt the eyes on me immediately. I remembered what my husband had told me about them being jealous, so I held my shoulders back, gave them my famous coy grin, and ordered a sausage biscuit with cheese and a carton of milk. It was the first time I ever ate store-bought food, and I ate it sitting on the steps out front. I sat for a bit, enjoying that sunny morning and thinking about the night before, just looking around at the people and wondered if all of them combined could be as happy as I was at that very moment.

"Lord, for the rest of my life," I said in a prayer, "sunny mornings will be my favorite time of day. 'Til the day I die, if I ever feel sad, I will think back to this very day. Blessed I will know I am each time the sun shines on my face. Thank you, God, for all you have given me. Amen."

I figured it was about time to head back to Daddy and Mama's house and since town wasn't much further from the house than the honky-tonk, I decided I'd walk back. Besides, I was in love and on top of the world and I wouldn't even notice how long the walk was. What I did notice as I got closer to the house was just how small it really was. I was a woman now, and I was ready for bigger and better things. The night before had proved my mama wrong. 'Doing it' was not as bad as she said it was. Maybe she was 'doing it' wrong. In any case, 'doing it' was never discussed again. I had found a new side to myself that night and I had every intention of keeping that feeling going.

I finally got home, but I didn't find everyone waiting happily for me. Never in a million years could I have been prepared for what I did find. As I walked the drive towards the house, there was a car parked next to my daddy's truck I had never seen before. Suddenly I felt butterflies again, for some reason I wanted to throw up. There was a large black man resting behind the wheel and his eyes darted towards me as I walked past the biggest car I had ever seen and around back of the house to where my daddy and mama were sitting with a woman a lot older than my mama. The woman was sitting with her back to me as I got closer. My mama had an odd look on her face and wouldn't look me in the face. Instead of a salutation, my daddy said, "Gail, come sit down, honey. We got something to talk to you about."

Honey? *Honey?* I knew right away that something was wrong because my daddy had never called me 'honey' in my life. It must be bad. Instead of sitting down like my daddy asked, I stood there as those butterflies in my stomach got worse.

"What's wrong? Who is she, Daddy?"

My mind went blank as he started to speak. "Gail—" But Daddy was stopped short as the old woman stood up and almost instinctively placed her purse over her arm as she reached for a pair of gloves.

"Mr. Martin, I am quite accustomed to handling my own

affairs, so allow me, please."

Before my daddy even had a chance to respond or halt the woman, she continued, "Gail, I am Maxwell's grandmother. My associates in town could not wait to tell me what they had heard, but quite honestly, I didn't believe it."

She never looked at me as, one by one, she pulled each glove over her small fingers, never interrupting what she came to say.

"Then, when Maxwell confirmed it this morning, I had to act immediately. This marriage was not, nor would it have been, approved by his family. So, I am sure you will understand why I found it necessary to make the proper arrangements to have this marriage annulled."

She was now strategically placing her hat and veil on her head, paying no mind to my feelings, as she continued, "Gail, I am quite sure you are a nice enough person, but, let's face it, child. The marriage would never work. Maxwell's family has many plans for him, and being married to, well, a person of lesser status is, for lack of better terms, not suitable."

I just stood there, not understanding what she was saying, let alone understanding what she was meaning. All I could do was watch her mouth move as she continued her verbal assault. Finally, she was satisfied that her hat was properly placed and she was sure she had made her point.

"That is all I came to say. I have already discussed this with Maxwell and he understands completely."

Then she directed the final dagger at my daddy.

"Mr. Martin, Maxwell sends his regrets, but, unfortunately, I... I mean, the family, asks that you not contact us...I mean, him in the future."

I just stood there, numb and not knowing what to say.

"Daddy? Mama? What did she mean, 'annulled'? Can somebody tell me what that means? Where is Max? I want to see him! What did you do to him?"

Of all the times in my life that I had needed my mama, this was the time. My mama stood up and came over to hug me. I still had no idea what Max's grandmother meant as Mama tried to explain to me.

"Child, annulled means he took it back. He didn't really mean it and he didn't want to marry you. Gail, honey, you are better off without that siditty family, anyway."

Seeing the look on my face, my daddy had listened to enough. He stood up, and trying hard to remember his religion, mustered up as much Southern charm as he could.

"Ma'am, if you've said your peace, I think it's high time you leave. We've got some repairin' to do with our daughter."

"Certainly, Mr. Martin, I can understand how this might affect her. After all, Maxwell does come from good stock, and I am sure he has made a very good impression on her. Just remember our chat, Mr. Martin. The Jackson family will not be responsible for any 'situations' that may arise from your daughter's indiscretions. As a businessman, yourself, I know you understand."

Max's grandmother did not even say good-bye. As she walked towards the car the driver opened the rear door and helped her in. Just as quick as she had blurted out her speech, they were driving away. I stood there, still numb and not knowing what I just heard. I watched the car throwing dust in the air behind it as it turned onto the road, leaving me speechless and without the very man I had just married and shared the best night of my life with. My young heart was broken and I just knew I would never get over it. I cried for weeks after that afternoon, and we never heard from Max's family again.

That, my children, is how The Soldier came into my life and just as quickly left.

# Chapter Four
## *Your Daddy*

MY MAMA AND DADDY HADN'T RAISED a quitter. After a couple of months, I started to feel better about myself and soon that urge to dance surfaced again. I thought that maybe I would feel better if I went back to the honky-tonk, so I would slip out some nights and head into town and dance for a while just to keep up on the new dances and the new songs. It was 1938, before I knew it, and I had just turned "sweet sixteen." I had mostly gotten over the painful words Maxwell's grandmother had thrown at me, but I never stopped thinking about Maxwell.

Daddy's tomato business continued to grow, but now there was a money shortage all over the place. Prices of everyday items had gone up so much that people all over the county had fallen on some times that looked likely to only get harder. The grown-ups were all talking about some man named Adolph Hitler who was causing a stir somewhere overseas and with talk of another war, President Roosevelt had put a stop to the furloughs. Since Brother wasn't able to come home, the rest of us kids had to help

Mama and Daddy around the house and fields as much as we could. Us kids had also started getting older by then and as the teenagers hormones kicked in, the girls were starting to think about looking good and none of the seven kids left at home were happy with the hand-me-downs anymore.

It was late on a warm Saturday evening in June of 1938. I snuck out again that evening, but it was mostly out of habit, this time because I didn't much feel like dancing. Instead, I just sat at one of the tables by the dance floor watching the other couples. I really wasn't even listening to the music, I was busy pondering the situation Mama and Daddy were in. I must have been way out in left field because I didn't notice when James Monroe came and sat next to me and placed a shot of whiskey and a pack of Lucky Strike cigarettes in front of me. He just sat there next to me, staring, with a big smile on his face.

When I realized he was sitting there, I gave him that coy, shy grin the men had come to recognize as mine.

"Where you at tonight, Gail? I ain't seen that much concentration on a face since my horse had her foal!"

I couldn't help but giggle. I picked up the glass, downed the shot, rubbed that sulfur-tipped match on the table and lit a cigarette.

"Jimbo, you know Calvin wasn't able to come home again, this summer and us seven kids are having to help Daddy in the fields. Well, they're havin' a hard time with money and I wish there was something I could do to help 'em out."

Jimbo listened to me for a few minutes, as if understanding everything I was saying. Jimbo knew my daddy and mama. He knew how hard Daddy and Mama worked in the fields and what good folks they were.

"Gail. I've known your folks a long time. I also know you are too young to be in here, and I promised your daddy I would keep my eye on you. Your pa is a proud man, and he would never go along with what I'm about to tell you, so you be sure and keep that in mind when you go telling your folks what I'm gonna say. You hearin' me?"

He bought another couple of drinks, and I was getting pretty relaxed. My head and shoulders were bobbing back and forth as The Andrews Sisters were singing, "Mama's little baby loves shortinen', shortinen', Mama's little baby loves shortinen' bread," and my feet were tapping at the base of the chair I was leaning back in.

"OK, Jimbo, you got my attention, what you trying to say?"

"Gail, honey, you are one of the most grown up little kids I ever met, and I ain't seen a heart as big as yours in a hundred moons. I know you truly want to help your folks out, so I am prepared to offer you the chance to make the money you want. If you are willing to help me out you can make enough money to help your folks and have some extra spending money of your own."

By now, I had stopped bouncing in my seat and had propped my elbows on the table facing him. Looking back on it, I must have been a sight, young as I was, sitting there with a cigarette hanging out of the corner of my mouth with both fists wrapped around yet another shot glass of whiskey.

"What you want me to do?"

I wasn't hearing the music any more. Jimbo had my curiosity going and I wanted to hear more about it.

"Come outside with me so we can talk a little more privately."

So, we got up, walked out that big red door and to the corner of the building. Jimbo explained to me that he and some other local boys had a business that was very lucrative but it was getting harder for them to get their deliveries done. He asked if I had ever heard of moonshine.

"Well, yeah! I wasn't born yesterday!"

He laughed at me, making some remark about my age and how I might not have been born yesterday, but I wasn't too from it. Anyway, he went on to explain about the woods back of the tomato fields my daddy owned and told me about people in other counties that knew how good their shine was. They had been making moonshine way before prohibition ended in 1933, but because the government was taxing liquors so bad, it was cheaper to buy it from them. They could make it fast enough, but they were having trouble getting it to them. They were beginning to have some run-ins with authorities in other counties and they needed a new face to help them out. The sheriff's office in Clayton County knew Jimbo and his boys and no one ever said anything to them about their deliveries. Besides, even though they would never admit it, they were all regulars of Jimbo's boys.

"And," Jimbo told me, "because they all know your pa, and because we been usin' the woods behind your pa's fields, they kind of look out for us around here."

Jimbo continued telling me about the job he had for me.

"Gail, the only thing you got to do is drive a car for us and deliver the food to people. I told your pa a long time ago that I was gonna watch out for you, so you won't have to collect any money, cause that can get dangerous. No, ma'am! All you got to do is ride up and down the roads when we have deliveries and watch out for the police."

I was so proud that he asked me to help him with his business and I felt like such a grown-up. I had been smoking cigarettes and drinking whiskey for years, I had already become a woman with Maxwell Jackson, and now I was being asked to help James Monroe and his boys with their business. No one was going to tell me I was a kid anymore! I told Jimbo I would be glad to do it, but I didn't have a car.

"Not a problem!" he said. "You come see me and the boys tomorrow and we will fix that!"

It was getting late, and I decided it was time for me to get home. Daddy and Mama had known I was sneaking out, but, out of respect for them, I never stayed real late because I knew there was work to do early the next day and I didn't want to disappoint them.

I don't think I slept at all that night, and I was really tired the next day. I couldn't wait until Sunday dinner was over and after I helped clean the dishes, I lay down across the bed the seven of us kids shared and fell asleep. Before I knew it, Little Stan woke me up breathing in my ear. I was so tired when I lay down that I didn't even hear any of them when they crawled in bed for the night. I lay there a few minutes remembering what Jimbo and I talked about, and I got excited. Not because I would soon be able to help Mama and Daddy with money, but because I was excited about my new job as a moonshine runner and the adrenaline was flowing in my veins for the first time in so long. I got that same excited feeling in my stomach the very first night I snuck out to the honky-tonk three years ago. I eased out of bed, got dressed, opened the back door, lifting it so it wouldn't creak, just like a million other times, and I took off down the dirt road towards the honky-tonk.

As I headed towards the door of the honky-tonk, I heard laughing coming from the side of the building and noticed three guys I had not seen before and one that looked kind of familiar, but I couldn't place him. They were standing around the shiniest car I had ever seen! It was a brand-new 1938 Ford Coupe, with big, black runners down each side of the car. I couldn't help but walk over to the car. I thought back on the promise to myself that first night at the honky-tonk that I was going to own a real pretty car one day, but I had now found a car that I liked even better than that one. The laughing stopped as I got closer and I noticed that the four men were looking at me as if I were interrupting them. That is when I saw Jimbo sitting in the driver's seat. He looked up at me and before even saying hello to me, he said, "Boys, say hello to Gail, your new running partner! Gail, meet your new friends!"

The three I did not know looked me over but didn't say anything; just nodded their heads with a kind of snarl. But the one I felt like I had met before smiled big and took off the hat he was wearing.

"Pleased to meet you! I know you may not remember me, little lady, but we met a few years ago, at what I understand was your first night at this fine establishment."

Then it hit me! I *did* remember him! He was the guy with the big strong arms who had helped me up when I fell off the table and watched over me until my daddy showed up!

We just stood there looking at each other for a few minutes. With his dark, wavy hair, and those dark eyes behind that beautiful skin, he reminded me so much of Maxwell Jackson. I was speechless for a minute.

"I can't get over how you've grown up," he told me. "I've known of you all your life, Gail, but I would not have thought you would turn out to be so pretty! Your mama and daddy must be proud."

My face turned red, but I couldn't tell if it was the flattery, or the hormones that stirred thinking back on becoming a woman with Maxwell. The likeness was uncanny. Jimbo knew about that situation and must have been able to tell what I was thinking because he brought me back to reality when he opened the car door and started telling the boys that I had agreed to do some of their "errands" for them. Two of them immediately objected to a girl helping them out, but after some coaxing from Jimbo, they finally agreed that maybe the authorities in the other counties wouldn't likely be looking for a woman to be running shine. They reluctantly welcomed me to the group and we all went in to have a drink.

We entered the building and headed towards a table large enough for all of us to sit. I made sure to sit next to the man that reminded me of Maxwell. We had been talking for almost an hour when he realized that he hadn't even introduced himself.

"Walter Payton Sanders, little lady, and the pleasure is all mine," he said, in a perfectly gentlemanly way. Even though he was nine years older than me, he knew my family well because he had grown up only a couple of miles down the road from the tomato fields my daddy owned. We talked, just the two of us, until the honky-tonk was about to close. When the lights came on in that old building, I knew I had been there too long and jumped up telling them all I had to run home. My new friends kind of elbowed each other and laughed.

"What's so funny? I ain't ever been out this late! My daddy is gonna be up in a few minutes and he's gonna be powerful angry!" Jimbo reached into his pocket and handed me a set of keys.

"Go on, Gail, drive yourself home." I reached my hand out by impulse and he dropped them in my hand.

"I can't do that, Jimbo, I ain't got a car. One of ya'lls gonna have to drive me home. And quick!"

In a million years, I never would have expected what he said next.

"You can drive a tractor, can't you? Well, it is almost the same thing. You turn it on, you give it gas, and you keep it straight on the road. If you're gonna work with us, you got to get used to driving. Go on. Take the keys. Besides, I got it for you to drive."

He took me by the hand and led me out to the parking lot and right over to that beautiful, new Ford Coupe with big black runners down the side. I was shocked speechless! The guys all stood and watched me staring at the car. I just knew he was going to tell me he was kidding, but then he opened the door for me, grabbed me by the hand, and guided me into the driver's seat of the car.

"Go, on! Crank it up!" Payton told me.

I had big tears in my eyes when, with shaking hands, I put the key in the ignition and turned it. "VVVVRROOOOM," the engine roared. It sounded like a hundred kittens all purring at the same time, and I was holding on to the steering wheel with both hands, just feeling that big new engine vibrating beneath me.

"Now, Gail, I know I should have got you out here earlier to look at it, so if you don't like it, one of the boys can drive it."

"NO!" was all I could think to say.

Payton offered to ride with me back home in case I got scared or had any questions about driving the car, but I felt like I had been born to drive that car. I had never seen anything that pretty up close and I never thought I would ever be sitting in something that looked like it came out of one of those magazine ads I had seen lying around the honky-tonk. I suddenly forgot the time and no longer thought about my daddy getting up any minute. I wanted to go and drive around. There was so much I wanted to see and do, and now I had a way to do it! But Payton and Jimbo talked me into waiting.

"Gail, honey, there's gonna be plenty of time behind the wheel of that car. Besides, it is late and you need to get some rest. You are gonna have a lot of explainin' to do to your ma and pa when they see this car parked in your yard tomorrow morning."

Jimbo was right. I had admired him for so long because he was so smart. If ever there was a "cat's meow," Jimbo was it.

"Just let Payton drive home with you to make sure you can drive it OK, then we can get you started on your first errand on Tuesday."

One of the boys followed behind us so he could pick Payton up after he got me back to the house. On the way home that night, after I got over that big smile on my face, Payton and I picked up the conversation as if we had never stopped. Even being older than me, he was easy to talk to and he enjoyed hearing me talk. I enjoyed hearing him talk, too. Only, when he spoke, I heard his voice, but I saw Maxwell's mouth moving. I knew from the start that I was going to have to be careful to not call him the wrong name. *Payton. His name is Payton,* I kept telling myself over and over again. Driving sure did beat walking and hitchhiking and it seemed like we barely left the honky-tonk before we got back to those tomato fields and that little four-room house sitting on those big rocks. I wanted to keep talking to Payton, but he reminded me that I had a long day ahead of me and I was going to need at least some rest.

*What a sweet, sweet man,* I thought as he got out of the car at the end of the driveway and got into the truck that had followed behind us.

All of a sudden, I did feel very tired. I wanted to be careful not to wake up the family, so I left the car parked on the road by the mailbox so I would make as little noise as possible. I slowly opened the door to my new Ford Coupe, and then just as slowly closed the door as I got out so it wouldn't slam. I kind of giggled because it was just like when I was sneaking out of the house. I took about ten steps away from the vehicle and I turned around to look at it. It was glowing in the bright June moonlight, and I had a huge smile on my face as I tiptoed up the steps to the back door with my usual ritual of lifting the door as I opened it. As I closed it behind me and slipped into the bedroom that kept getting smaller every time I came back to it, I realized more and more that I was turning into an adult.

I barely remember lying down, and I definitely don't remember closing my eyes. The next thing I heard was the sound of my mama and my oldest sister Tina getting breakfast on the table. Daddy was talking to someone out on the front porch. I knew that voice. It was Payton. He had come by the house to speak to my daddy. I couldn't tell what they were talking about, but it was the same look on their faces as they had the night I was hauled back from my dancing debut at the honky-tonk.

Payton got in his truck and was almost out onto the street when Daddy came in the front door yelling my name.

"Gail Leighann Martin! Get up and come out to the table! I got a couple of questions you need to answer!"

I figured he was mad, because he never used my full name for anything. Daddy shooed away the other six kids and he and Mama sat down at the table with me.

"Gail, I understand you got something to tell me about that new car parked out by the mailbox."

I swallowed nervously.

"Yes, sir. I do."

I knew better than to lie to either of them because Mama could look at us and somehow know if we were telling the truth. I truly wished I knew what Payton had said to him, so I didn't make one or the other of us look like a fool.

"Gail, I been knowin' since you was 13 that you been sneakin' out at night. You always been hardheaded, and no matter what we said or did, you was gonna do it anyway. You never slacked up on your workload, so I just looked the other way about it most of the time. But that Sanders boy has been man enough to tell me what you was planning on doin'."

I was afraid I was about to get a good whoopin'. After all, I was only 16 and I was still under their roof. I kept listening.

"With your brother away, you have helped me and your mama

a whole lot around here, but I'm thinking I may have put too big a load on your shoulders. When I told you I needed you around here, I meant with the chores. Gail, your mama and I never wanted to make you feel like you kids needed to help out with money."

I listened, almost relieved, as he told me that he had long known of Jimbo, Payton, and the others, as well as the moonshine stills in the back woods. He also let me know that Payton told him I was going to help them with their deliveries.

"Gail, I found out a long time ago that I can't stop you from doing what you want to do once you set your mind to doing it. I don't condone anything you are about to do, but I understand why you are wantin' to do it. I know all the boys you been hanging around, and Payton swears to me that they will take care of you. I s'pose if you're gonna do this, you got a good bunch of guys in your corner. They must think a lot of you if they bought you that purdy new car out by the mailbox."

I felt more at ease as he talked, because I was so sure he was going to whoop the tar out of me. Mama didn't let on much as Daddy continued.

"Before you get behind the wheel, I want to make sure you know how to drive."

I was shocked when he told me to grab my keys.

"We're gonna start by goin' up and down East Fayetteville Road."

Daddy showed me about putting gas in the car, changing tires, and even adding oil in case it got low. That day was one of the only days in my life that I almost forgot he was my daddy. That day, for just a minute, I thought about him not as a tall, hard-nosed, mean old man, but as a caring friend. Of course, it didn't last for long, because it wasn't long until he brought me back to reality when he barked, "OK, time to go home. There's too much to get done if you're 'bout to be gone all the time."

The tomato fields in June are at a critical time. All those horrible acres of plants had little blooms on them, and with those blooms came the bugs and the worms Mama and Daddy made us pick off before they ate too much of the plant. They were good for fishin', but I hated the sight of them. The rest of the afternoon, we all walked the rows, and when it was time for dinner, Mama didn't have to tell us twice to come in and eat. Looking back on it now, I really enjoyed those days. It sure did help me get through the rest of my life. Hard work never hurt nobody, and we were all the better for it.

So, girls, that is how I met your daddy.

# Chapter Five
## *The Lord Giveth, the Lord Taketh Away*

FOR THE NEXT YEAR, MY VISITS to the honky-tonk were less frequent. I would spend most of the day working in the fields with Mama, and most evenings were spent keeping the roads of Clayton, Henry, Fulton, and Heard counties hot, as I delivered moonshine to some of the most surprising homes. From very prominent people to very common people, they all anxiously waited for the smoothest moonshine Georgia ever tasted, and probably has since. During this time, Payton and I spent many hours together talking and getting to know each other. He held his word to my daddy and really watched over me, making sure that the car I was driving was in top shape all the time, and making sure that he knew everywhere I was headed. He would be the one to load up the trunk when I left, and he would make sure to be there when I got back, just to make sure I made it home. On the weekends, as a reward for the hard work I had done all week, Payton would take me to the honky-tonk and sit at one of the tables next to the dance floor and watch me as I listened and danced to the newest song on the old Wurlitzer. I grew to respect Payton and I just knew he would be a good provider for me. Soon, my feelings even turned to a kind of love for him.

It was 1939. I was still a child in the eyes of my parents, but no one could deny that I had become quite a woman. Then, in mid-August, God sent me the biggest test of faith I had seen in my 17-year-old life. It was raining steady, and too muddy to go into the fields, so I had decided to go by myself and get a drink. I put my dime into the jukebox and a few of us were leaning on the bar singing along with Gene Autry as he crooned "Back in the Saddle Again." I had thrown my head back to down my third shot of whiskey and, as I looked up into the mirror behind the bar, I felt my heart stop. Maxwell walked into the bar! Suddenly, I was 13 years old again, and every feeling I thought I had gotten over overwhelmed me and I just knew I was about to pass out! I was no longer aware of where I was. The music and the noise became just a faint whisper in the back of my mind. As if living it for the first time, I was standing at the top of a creaky staircase at that hotel in town, my husband of only a few hours opening the door to that tiny room and my womanhood.

Maxwell's term in the service had ended and he had decided to come home. The plans his grandmother had made for him to run the family business were happening just as she planned. He had only been home a few days, just long enough to gather some of his friends together for a drink or two. Brother had decided to stay in the service and re-enlisted for another term. No matter, for whether it was anger at what Maxwell did to his little sister before and after our short-lived marriage, or what Maxwell's grandmother said to Daddy and Mama, the two men barely spoke anymore. Maxwell never even tried to contact Brother to let him know he was going back home.

After four years, Max looked a bit older, but not in a bad way. He was more beautiful than I remembered, with the same dark eyes that sparkled like diamonds, and the same naturally curly hair that accentuated the wonderfully tanned skin. As he entered the bar, our eyes locked onto each other and we both stood there, neither of us saying anything in what was a most awkward moment.

"Gee, you look pretty, Gail."

He broke the wonderful silence that, though only seconds long, was enough to bring back every emotion I had fought to hide over the past years. Never since had I felt such a pull towards another man. Girls, you would hope to one day love someone as much as I loved Maxwell Jackson—my man in uniform. At that very moment, my wedding night, and the journey Max had taken me on raced through my mind and I just knew he was the reason that God had created me. As the music and the noise slowly crept back into my mind, I remembered where I was. I also remembered why I came to the honky-tonk and the only thing I could think to say was, "Hello."

I felt stupid for even opening my mouth, but I was so full of emotions that I couldn't think of anything smarter or wittier to say. I even forgot to flash my famous coy little grin. Maybe he, too, was embarrassed, or maybe Maxwell must have thought I was still upset at him. In any case, he was looking a bit deflated by how our reunion began.

"Well, I'll let you get back to your friends. It is really good to see you, Gail."

My mind still not completely functioning, all I could muster up to say was "Thank you."

*Thank you? Thank you? How dumb was that?* My pride kicked in as I turned my back to him and walked back over to my friends at the bar. I picked up my drink and looked at myself in the big plate glass mirror behind the counter. "Thank you" kept going through my mind over, and over again, like I was stuck in first gear and couldn't adjust the clutch for second. I had completely lost the mood for being there and I suddenly felt totally alone and sad, just like I felt when that big car carried Maxwell's grandmother down the road from my house. I didn't even finish my drink. I just turned and walked out of the honky-tonk. The door had just closed behind me and I had only taken about four steps out of the building when I heard it open again quickly.

"Gail! Gail! Wait!"

It was Maxwell. He grabbed me by the arm and swung me around.

"Gail, I have thought about you every day for the past four years. You will never know how hard it was for me to get over the emptiness in my heart. But, you gotta understand why I had to do what my family said."

I listened to him as he rambled on and on about the business his family owned, and the expectations they had of him. He apologized a thousand times. I wanted to stay mad at him, but the look on his face and those dark sparkling diamonds I was looking into melted me. I was leaning on the back of my car, not really looking at him as he spoke. I was somewhere between a heartbroken little girl and a jaded woman who had been all but left at the altar. He must have seen that part of me, because he stopped talking, reached over with both hands, and, as softly as when he sat beside me on the bed the night we made love, he held my face and gently kissed me on the lips. That was all it took to drown all my doubts and re-ignite my love.

Like a broken dam, my hormones raged and I melted into his arms. Since it was raining and we had nowhere else to go, we got into my car and drove down to the fishing pond. I knew there wouldn't be anyone there and it would be a good place to talk. We had a lot of catching up to do as I told him what all I had been doing since he was gone. I told him how I got the car and about the "errands." We talked about our families, and I even asked him how his grandmother had been. I didn't really care, but I asked anyway.

We had been sitting for a long time and the windows were all fogged up. I am not sure how long we had been there, but it had stopped raining, so we rolled the windows down to let the car air out.

"I need to get back home now, Max. I know the family is going to wonder where I've been. I am sure it is dinnertime and Daddy likes us all to be sitting at the table together. When can I see you again?" I waited for his reply.

"For the rest of my life, as far as I can see, Gail."

Besides the night Jimbo told me to, "Go on! Crank it up," that was the best thing anyone had ever said to me in my life. Max and I ended up making love right there in my car, right alongside the fishing pond down the road from where my mama had told me her version of the birds and the bees. That was the first of many times to come that we would sneak off and fulfill our mutual desires. He told me his family would still not accept his decision, so we had to sneak around at night to be together. During that time, I continued to spend most of my days with Payton and I began to feel guilty about the double life I was leading. To add to that guilt, Payton shocked me one afternoon by expressing his undying love for me.

He told me that he couldn't hide it anymore and that I should stop trying to ignore it. He told me how frustrating it was to see me every day, watching me dance around like I did, and then go home alone, feeling his heart breaking because he never had the nerve to tell me how he felt. Over the years, in my heart I had known. I had caught him looking at me with those eyes that reminded me of Maxwell's. I even took for granted that he enjoyed my company and I was surprised that he had taken so long to tell me. Everyone that saw us together also knew it. So, whether from an underlying feeling of love for him, or maybe just guilt for having acted on the feelings I had for Maxwell, that afternoon I took the strong, older man, who had suddenly turned into a lovesick little boy, into my arms and we made love. From that mid-August when Maxwell came back into my life, I was leading a life that some people might think promiscuous. I had Payton during the day and Maxwell at night, and I felt like I had it all.

Maxwell took care of everything I *wanted*. He treated me like the queen he always said I should be. He would bring me flowers every night we were together. He would say sweet things to me the whole time we were together, and *every* time we were together, we would end up making mad passionate love together. Payton made sure to take care that I didn't *need* for anything and made sure I had everything. He was, indeed, the provider I always knew he would be, including making love to me with such sweetness and tenderness. However, lovemaking was just as fulfilling as it was with Payton, but in a different way. I was completely satisfied with my double life and I had the world on a chain.

Until the chain got caught up in the wheels of life. I turned 18 in January and the worst thing that had ever happened to me changed everything in my life. I had missed my period. At first, I thought it was just late because I was so tired from all my carousing around. After all, I was on the go all the time. Between my days with Payton and my nights with Maxwell, I only slept a few hours every night and I really was tired. It started with a queasy feeling some mornings, but in a few days, I woke up every morning really sick. In the back of my mind, I knew what was happening, but just to be safe, I never let anyone know I was sick. I would just go "for a walk" in the mornings when the kids were all getting ready for school so my mama wouldn't see me because I knew she would know right off the bat that I was expecting. After all, after already bearing eight kids of her own she knew what morning sickness looked like. The morning sickness finally ended, but my period never started. I finally accepted the fact that I was pregnant, but not knowing what to do, I never told anyone. I kept thinking about the conversation I had with Mama before I went to be with Max. It was as if she was screaming into my ears how dirty sex was with a man and a woman, all the while thinking about how wrong she was.

There I was, 18 years old, pregnant, not married, and completely unsure who the father was. I spent the next couple of weeks acting like nothing was wrong with me, all the while taking careful notice of both the men in my life. Payton was a strong man, and I looked up to him almost as much as I did my daddy. I was sure he would make a wonderful provider for the baby and me. On the other hand, the heat and passion flowing between Maxwell and me made me want him so deeply. I was certain that the man who I married almost 5 years ago was the father. *Yes, it has to be Maxwell's baby.* So, I made the decision to tell Maxwell I was going to have his baby.

For a January night, it was unusually warm, so I decided to walk down the road to meet him instead of driving as I had many times in the past months. But, instead of immediately starting to embrace him, I looked at him and told him I had something serious to talk about.

"Max. You're gonna be a daddy."

In my mind, I had created a beautiful scene of him smiling very big and taking me into his arms, holding me as we both expressed a wonderful love for each other. I had imagined the plans we would make to get married again; and, and in my mind, had already pick out the house we would live in to raise what would be the first of our children. In my mind, I had already decorated my little kitchen in white lace curtains and matching towels, and imagined myself cooking breakfast, lunch and dinner for my husband and our baby's daddy. Oh, how perfect my life was going to be! I was going to show my mama that life was not the same as she had detailed for me, and, finally, Maxwell's grandmother was going to accept me as part of the family. I was going to be completely happy.

I never even imagined his reaction. You'd have thought I had thrown hot water in his face! His body stiffened up, he pushed me away from him and shouted, "WHAT THE HELL? WHAT DO YOU TAKE ME FOR? YOU DON'T THINK IT'S MINE, DO YOU?"

I was dumbstruck. I could not believe my ears. I didn't feel anything. I couldn't hear anything. Surely I misunderstood what he just said.

"YOU LITTLE TRAMP, YOU PLANNED THIS, DIDN'T YOU? My grandmother was right about you. I should have left you back at the lake as soon as I slept with you!"

Surely it wasn't true. Suddenly, I felt as cheap as a penny's worth of candy. All this time, Maxwell had made me believe that he loved me. Now, I found out that he only wanted me for my body. Right at that very minute, I felt dirtier than I had ever before and ever since. Max stood up, and without even saying good-bye, left me sitting under that old oak tree that had been "our spot under the stars" since we started seeing each other again, not so long ago. Sad was not an ample word. Hurt was not even enough to say. Hollow was more appropriate. I sat and cried under the same stars I had made love to the night before. I wondered what to do. The love I thought I had was nothing more than sinful lust.

I was not going to think about giving up, and I was sure that Payton would be more understanding. Payton was older and more mature. Surely, he would understand the situation I was in. However, telling him I was pregnant would not be the issue with him. Telling him about Maxwell was my concern. I had to think of something soon, because to my mama and daddy nothing in life would be more humiliating than their already uncontrollable daughter having a child out of wedlock. Surely, Payton would want to do the right thing and want to marry me and take care of things. By the time I got home I had already made myself believe that everything would be fine and that Payton would accept being the father of the baby.

The next day I met up with Jimbo, Payton, and the boys like any other day, only I made sure I got Payton alone. He was absolutely clueless about the baby and I felt sure that I had managed to keep Max a secret from Payton as well.

"Payton, I got something to tell ya, but I need to you listen to me closely."

I thought back on the way I told Maxwell and I thought maybe I needed to use a little of that "coy little girl" on him that he had grown to love. Payton stopped what he was doing and took his hat off to sit next to me on an old log that had been there so long the bark had worn off, leaving shiny spots like car seats, the same size as the men's behinds.

"What's on your mind, little lady? You got a powerful serious look on your face."

As he sat there, I considered every action he took. He was definitely a strong man, the lines on his face strewn with wisdom that suddenly showed his age. I suddenly got very nervous and was about to change my mind about telling him, but something in me told me to go on and say it.

"I'm gonna have a baby, Payton."

I closed my eyes and waited for his reaction to be the same as I got from Maxwell.

"So, what you gonna do, Gail? You know what your folks is gonna say."

I thought, *Well, that went better than I thought. I might as well tell him the whole truth.* Although about an hour later, I was wishing I had held back on the whole truth.

I told him about Brother's friend from the service and I described how we had fallen so much in love. I told him about Maxwell's grandmother, and tried to describe how hard a broken heart was to get over. Payton didn't let on about anything while I talked. The guys were ragging him about getting back to work, but they could tell by the look on his face that we were in a very serious conversation so they let him be. I would love to have been able to read his mind because he wasn't looking at me anymore, and I couldn't see his eyes. Finally, I nervously explained about the day I was at the bar when Max walked in the door. I was stumbling, trying to find words.

"Um, I, uh, we kind of started seeing each other again."

I saw Payton's head swing around at me and his eyes looked straight into my soul while I finished my sentence.

"And I…ugh…we…mmm…"

"YOU'VE BEEN SLEEPING WITH HIM, HAVEN'T YOU?"

I suppose I had done a good job of hiding my relationship with Maxwell all this time. Payton never had a clue that I had been double timing him.

"WHERE DOES THE ASSHOLE LIVE? I WANT TO KNOW SO I CAN BEAT THE HELL OUT OF HIM! I CAN'T BELIEVE HIM! I CAN'T BELIEVE YOU! I CAN'T BELIEVE THIS! DAMN! HOW COULD I BE SO STUPID"

"Payton, I never meant to hurt you! You gotta believe me!

This wasn't supposed to happen!"

Payton turned and walked away from me, and I was right behind him, begging him to stop.

"Wait, Payton! Let's talk about this. Maxwell doesn't matter to me! I want *you* to be the father of my baby!"

By now, all the guys had stopped what they were doing and all of them were standing watching the show unveil.

"See, I *told* you things was gonna go wrong!" one of them said.

Jimbo, in an attempt to provide a little privacy for us, shouted back, "Shut up, boy! This ain't none of your concern! Keep your mind to your tendin'!"

Payton got in his truck and drove off, leaving me in the late January chill, alone and with child. I was not even aware of the stares the other guys were throwing at me. At that very moment, I had no clue what to do. Both men in my life had turned their back on me. I knew my mama had raised me better than this, and God was punishing me for being a loose woman. Jimbo told me it would be best in my condition if I took some time off. He suggested I swallow my pride and go home so my mama could help me get through the decisions I had to make.

*Home. Yeah, I guess that is all I have left. Home. Won't this be fun? Hi, Mom! I'm home! Oh, by the way, I'm pregnant and I have no idea who the daddy is. Yeah. Home.* I let out a huge sigh and suddenly I felt the chilly January air. I got in my car and headed home to face the music.

Remember me telling you that Mama could look at us and tell when we were telling the truth? Well, when I got home, I found her at home by herself. The other kids had gone to school and Daddy had gone on another of those trips he'd been taking lately. He would be gone for days at a time, and he was very secretive about where he went and, if Mama knew, she never let on. As soon as I walked in the door, Mama took one look at my face and said, "Gail Leighann Martin, come sit down, we got to talk."

I felt shamed even being in the house with her because of what I had to tell her, but I did as she said and I sat down at the little table that the grown-ups ate at and got ready to lay it all out.

"You may have been fooling most of them around ya, but you ain't fooled me any. I brung you into this world and I can tell by the way you say hello when something is wrong. What's done happened?"

I just sat there, a few feet away from the old cook stove, with my arms folded over my chest, clinching my sweater over me like I was freezing to death. I couldn't look at her. I had to laugh when she knocked her knuckles on the table leg near the chair I was sitting in and said, "SPEAK ASS! MOUTH WON'T!"

I started crying as I told my mama all about the last few months of my life and how much of a shamble I had made of things. I expected her to get a hickory after me, but I was surprised to find her less upset and more compassionate.

There hadn't been too many times in my life before then that I needed my mother, but it sure was nice to have her that day. I was glad that no one else was home because it gave me and Mama a lot of time to talk. We were like two grown women instead of a mother and a daughter. By the time the kids were getting home from school, I felt better about things and my mama had convinced me that we were family and that we would get through it together. I never knew how or even what Mama told Daddy about my predicament. Daddy never said a word to me. I always wondered if he was just too embarrassed or maybe he was so ashamed that he could never say anything. In any case, nothing much was said about it by anyone in the family. It was just "one of those things families share."

That was probably the longest summer of my life. I never left the yard, and Mama and Daddy didn't have any visitors. Mama said she knew by the way I was carrying it that the baby was going to be a girl, and it was going to be soon. Sure enough, but not too soon for me, on October 23, 1940, in that little house on Flat Shoals Road, I gave birth to baby girl. It was a couple of days before I even knew what to name her, but it was time to fill out the birth certificate and get her registered with the state, so I had to find a proper name for her. I had no problem with the address. I had even decided her name was going to be Addy Mae. But what about a last name? When I looked down at the little life I held in my arms, I couldn't help but see how much she looked like Maxwell Jackson with her deep toned skin and her dark curly hair. But, I also saw a resemblance to Payton. After all, Payton had reminded me of Maxwell from the start.

To save my family any further humiliation, I decided to write "S-A-N-D-E-R-S" in the section for the last name. It really tore me up inside not knowing, but I figured Payton Sanders would be a good name for my baby to accept as her daddy. Yet, the more I looked at little Addy Mae, the more I wanted Maxwell to see her.

*Surely,* I thought, *surely he would fall in love with her as I have and want to be her daddy.* That afternoon, I wrote a letter to Maxwell and asked him to please come and see her. "I got sumthin' to tell ya," was all I wrote. Little Stan took it to the mailbox for me and I stood at the window until I saw the mailman pick it up from the box and carry it away with him. I thought several times about running out and getting it from the box and stop it from going, but just as I had about decided to go get it, the mailman came around and got it. It was too late. All I could do now was wait.

Addy Mae was only a few weeks old, but was already so very beautiful. I truly was lucky to have her. As soon as your Aunt Lizzie heard that Addy Mae had been born, she made arrangements for one on her neighbors to bring her to visit. Lizzie stood in amazement at the little wonder that God had put into my life. Addy Mae's fingers were clinched in little fists, one in her little mouth, and the other reaching behind her ear like she was stretching. Her perfect, bronze toned skin was so smooth you couldn't help but want to touch it. Her hair was so thick and curly as it stuck out from under the homemade quilt I had her wrapped up in. Seeing my sister-in-law standing there looking at my baby made me very proud, and I became more determined that once Maxwell saw this little angel that he would fall in love with her. But, I had just about figured the letter I sent him was either lost or had been thrown away.

For November, it was actually a nice day, and I had been

rocking little Addy Mae in my arms on the back stoop when I heard a car coming up the driveway. It was Maxwell! He had gotten my letter, after all! I placed Addy Mae on a pallet on the ground next to the porch and was standing there with my hands on my hips when he got out of the car. As he got out, he wasn't smiling much at all. It was more the kind of greeting you would give a stranger you meet on the street.

"Max! I am *so* glad to see you! I was afraid the letter I sent you got lost or something!"

"Hello, Gail," he said, still barely smiling. "How are you?"

I was a bit taken aback, because, once again, his reaction was not what I had imagined. I had been walking towards him but stopped when I felt the coldness in his voice.

"Max, I've missed you. I have someone I want you to meet. It's your little girl."

He started yelling so loudly that Addy Mae started crying.

"WHY DID YOU SEND FOR ME? HUH? TO SHOW ME THIS BABY? I ALREADY TOLD YOU, GAIL MARTIN, IT'S NOT MINE! YOU'RE CRAZY IF YOU THINK YOU ARE GOING TO GET ANY HELP OUT OF ME!"

With those words, he jerked the door to his car open, jumped in, cranked the car, jerked it into reverse, and spun rocks behind him as he jerked the car in gear and sped down the driveway and back onto the road. Gone, just like before. I was crushed by my Maxwell for the second time. Only, this time was worse. It was final. I never saw him again, and I was, once again, unwed and left alone.

From that day forward, I was determined to be a better mother. I had gambled on Maxwell twice and both times I had lost. I was determined to hold my head high regardless of my current situation. I got back in touch with Jimbo, but he was kind of hesitant to let me get back to work because I was a mother now.

"Now, Gail, I am thinkin' you might better stay home with the youngin' for a spell. Things has changed a bit since you become a mother. It's too dangerous for you to be leavin' your little girl without a mama."

Jimbo's words really cut me because I wanted so desperately to get back to a normal life. It had been over a month since the baby was born, and surely, she was old enough for my mama and sisters to watch while I was gone. Besides, Addy Mae got to where she cried a lot, lately, more than any of my brothers and sisters ever did when they were babies. Besides, I was getting real tired of never going out anymore.

I asked Mama if she would watch the baby for the night so I could go dancing. Mama told me, "I told you being a grown-up was different! Don't you make this a habit, Gail! I done raised my kids!"

I thanked Mama as I left for town, still driving my beautiful Ford Coupe. It wasn't quite as shiny as it used to be, but it was still the most beautiful thing on the road to me! Since I had not been working since the baby was born, I had no money, so when I got to the honky-tonk I got one of the locals to buy me a drink and I bummed a Lucky Strike from another. I felt right at home there. Since I became a mother, I was sure I would have missed out on some major changes in the jukebox. I was glad to see that nothing much had changed, and I was happy to just be in the place and listening. I didn't feel like dancing as much as I thought I would, so I just sat there and listened, drank, and smoked. I was deep in thought and I didn't notice when a drink was placed in front of me.

"Uh-hmph."

The sound of someone clearing a throat in my ear brought me out of my thought. I looked up, kind of irritated that someone was interrupting the only "me" time I had been able to get in many months. But, to my surprise, it was Payton. He had seen me walk in and had been watching me.

"How are you, Gail?"

"Fine, Payton, how are you?"

I thanked him for the drink as he sat down. I was not really sure what humiliation he was going to put me through. In fact, I didn't really care. I was away from home for a minute and enjoying the music.

"How's Addy Mae?" His question took me by surprise.

"I'm surprised you know her name."

"Gail," Payton said low, "I know you've been through a bad time in your life."

I sat and watched the others dance.

"And how would you know? I haven't heard from you since you left me at the still."

"I never went far. I been keeping tabs on you through your daddy."

I looked down at my almost empty glass, glanced over at him, then back at my glass, and then back at him, with a coy little grin. He took the hint and almost laughed as he asked the bartender for another shot. He offered me another cigarette, but, as if he owed it to me, instead of one from the pack, I took the whole pack and placed it on the table in front of me. He had turned his chair around beside me and propped himself on his elbows. We didn't talk much for the next few minutes. Instead, we looked at opposite directions of the honky-tonk. But that silence didn't stop me from thinking and as the wheels of my mind were turning quickly, I soon determined that I might just get my man after all. *How convenient! Addy Mae needs a daddy and as far as the state of Georgia knew, Payton was her daddy.* I was kind of scared to start talking to him again, because of the way our last conversation ended. I was actually thankful when he spoke first instead. Even though he didn't mention seeing Addy Mae, I was so happy to hear him ask to see me that I quickly agreed when he asked if he could see me again.

I figured it was about time for me to get back home. I was grateful that my mama was sitting for me, but I didn't want to take a chance on her getting mad at me. Besides, with Addy Mae crying so much now, I knew Mama's nerves would be worn and I thought I might need to relieve her, so I made plans to meet Payton the next day. I was going to bring him his lunch at the stills before he went on his afternoon "errands." When I got home, I was pleasantly surprised to see Mama sitting at the kitchen table cutting up some potatoes for dinner. It was actually quiet in the house and Mama held her finger to her lips as to shush me.

"Where's Addy Mae, Mama?"

"She's in there on my bed. I saw she had a bellyache, so I gave her something for colic. She has it pretty bad. Ain't too uncommon for a baby her age to get it. I just gave her a little bicarbonate. She went to sleep about an hour ago."

I was young, Addy Mae was my first baby, and no one told me about things like colic. No one ever told me there would be so much feeding and diaper changing, and crying, and, well, there was just so much I never counted on. I would have to remember that, though—"bicarbonate." It never occurred to me to ask how much to give her. *It can't be much; she isn't a very big baby. I'll figure it out later.*

For the next few weeks, I spent as much time as I could with Payton. Mostly at night at the honky-tonk. I didn't want to keep pawning Addy Mae off on Mama and my sisters, so I would stay home with her during the day and would slip out at night when everyone was asleep. Soon, Payton and I were sleeping together again, and I was trying to balance being a mother and being with Payton. Payton would ask about the baby now and again, but would rarely make time to see her. He never accepted her as his, but he did accept her as mine, and I thought that was an excellent start. As far as I was concerned, I *finally* had the good life I had hoped I would.

However, it didn't last much longer. Addy Mae never stopped crying. Instead, it got worse. Even the bicarbonate my mama gave her only lasted a few hours, and soon she would be crying again. Mama said it was time we got her to the doctor, but back then all we had was an old country doctor that made rounds in the county. The closest hospital was all the way in downtown Atlanta, and Daddy would be awfully mad if we spent money without asking him first. He had already been gone for a few days and we were sure he would be home soon. Hopefully, we could wait a little longer.

I was getting really scared because of her crying so much, and no matter how many times I rocked her, or how many times Mama and I swapped her back and forth, she cried louder and louder. Then she just stopped crying completely. That scared me even worse. I held her in my arms and watched her little face turn an odd color. She was barely breathing.

"OH MY GOD, MAMA! SOMETHING IS BAD WRONG!" I grabbed the baby's blanket and my keys. "I CAN'T WAIT ANYMORE FOR DADDY TO COME HOME. I AM TAKING HER TO THE HOSPITAL NOW!"

There was panic on Mama's face, a fear I had never seen before as she held her Bible against her chest. "GO ON, GAIL! TAKE HER TO EGLESTON HOSPITAL. WE SHOULD HAVE TAKEN HER BEFORE NOW!"

I drove as fast as I could down to the main road into downtown Atlanta. I thought I would never get there. I was holding Addy Mae in one arm while managing to change gears and drive with the other until I finally got to the hospital and pulled up to the front entrance. I jumped out, leaving the car, the keys, and everything right where it was.

The doctor on duty ushered us into a room and pulled her from my arms. One of the nurses made me sit down in a chair next to the bed. It was too late. My little angel, Addy Mae had died on the way to the hospital that night. I didn't know what to do. Like too many times before, I felt a hollow feeling. I sat there for the longest time. I just stared at my little baby on that gurney, and for the first time in her life, I heard how silent and peaceful she could be. I missed her already. I stood up, walked over to her, grabbed her into my arms, and cried. In a second, the security guard was standing at the door. He had seen what happened and went to move the car into a parking spot. He placed my keys on the end of the gurney, then silently stepped back out of the room.

It was a few minutes later when Mama came in the room. She had sent one of the kids to the woods behind the house to find some help. Jimbo happened to be there, and was more than obliged to bring Mama to the hospital. Both of them came into the room with a look of hope in their face. They knew what happened as soon as they looked at me. Mama always knew by looking in my eyes. She walked over to me and put her arms around me. It was the second time I truly felt that I needed my mama. Jimbo just stood beside us, holding his old hat over his heart, and said a prayer that the angels carry the new life home.

There was some paperwork to fill out, but because it was so late and because of what I had been through that night, the nurse said I could come back the next day and finish the papers. Jimbo told me to leave my car there at the hospital that evening and he would bring me back after I had gotten some rest. He carried me and Mama home and escorted us into the house. The other kids were up waiting for us to see what happened but Mama shooed them to bed and told them we would speak the next day. Instead of lying down with the other kids, Mama took me to her bed and I lay down next to her. I thought about what a crappy day it had been, and I started to cry. I fell asleep with my mama running her fingers through my hair and rubbing my shoulders, singing "Amazing Grace" softly in my ear, and up 'til the day I died, I never forgot "how sweet the sound."

The next day, we went to the hospital to finalize the paperwork. The attending doctor asked where the father was and when he found out that he wasn't available, he looked at me with a funny look.

"Oh. I understand," was all he said.

So, I had to sign all the papers myself. There was a paper that said something about an autopsy. The coroner report listed the death as "TOXEMIA." It was attributed to an overdose of bicarbonate in the stomach. They asked me several questions like, "How long had she been sick?" "How much bicarbonate did I give her?" and, "Why wasn't she brought to see a doctor?" By the time the doctor finished asking me all the questions, I felt just as dirty as I had felt the day I found out I was pregnant. I couldn't wait to get home.

The next thing to do was find a place to bury my baby. Mama and Daddy belonged to Pleasant Grove Church in Riverdale, so that was where we thought she should be buried. However, because Addy Mae was born out of wedlock, the elders in the church had declined burying the baby in the family plots.

"Because," one of them explained, "we have other church members to think of. It was not appropriate that the child was brought into this world in such a manner; therefore, it was not appropriate to send her out in a proper fashion. Granted, she was a child of God, but she was not a sanctioned part of the family. Therefore, we will allow her to be buried here, but not with the rest of the family."

The elders of the church were nice enough to "give" my mama a small plot of land a few hundred feet away from the rest of the family. We hired some of the old guys that hung out by the old Riverdale Barber Shop to dig a hole big enough to bury the little box that contained her little body.

It was a very small ceremony, with just the family members and the men who dug her grave for us. Even if the elders at the church would have allowed a tombstone, we could not afford one, and no one, not even Payton, would help us buy one. Most of the town felt that it must have been God's will that I not have her, and I was fighting hard to keep from feeling the same thing. *But*, I told myself, *I promised I was going to be a better mother, and I am going to be as good as my word.*

I went back to the grave a couple of days later with a couple of rocks from the back yard that daddy had pulled out of the field. I got the biggest ones little Stan and I could carry, and together we placed them at the head and foot of my Addy Mae's grave. "Now I will always know where she is," I told Stan, and I planned on visiting her as often as I could. He and I stood there beside my little angel, and I laid my head on his shoulders while I cried. He held the hands that sat on top of his young shoulders and told me, "It's OK, Gail. You can let go now."

He was there for me that day, just as he would be so many more times in our lives. That is why I loved my little brother Stan, and why, as I lay there the day I died, I held onto life until he got there. I had to hear him tell me it was "OK to let go."

# Chapter Six
## *Back in the Saddle*

AFTER THAT DAY, I WASN'T MUCH good for anything. In fact, I went into a deep depression that lasted for weeks. Since there wasn't a television in our house, and Daddy had, so far, refused to spend the money for a radio, there was nothing for us to do but entertain ourselves. The kids played outside when it wasn't too cold, or raining, or, back in the days when it snowed more than it does now, the kids used to go outside and build snowmen. Mama tried to make it fun for them by making snow cream using some milk and sugar and a little of the vanilla flavoring she kept in the pantry. When there was nothing else for us to do, Mama had us girls sitting around making quilts. I enjoyed that and had gotten very good at it. It was good therapy for me, and the kids used to read to me the things they were learning in school. My sisters would talk to me about the boys at school and my Little Stan would make the funny faces about them as young boys will.

Payton asked to see me on several occasions but I turned

down the invitation. I just wanted to be alone with my family. Daddy came to me one afternoon and told me it was high time I got on with my life.

"All is as it should be, Gail. We ain't the ones to be questionin' God's plan. It's time you got out of the house. I never thought I'd say this, but maybe you should get out to the honky-tonk and dance a jig or two."

It sounded so funny coming from my daddy that I had to giggle.

"There's that grin I got used to seein'! Now, get a move on. I know there's at least one man down there been waitin' for you for weeks."

I knew he was talking about Payton. I thought about it for a few minutes and I realized that I did need to get out and stretch my legs. *Besides*, I said to myself, *I am probably getting behind in the latest dance moves.*

Daddy was right. It did feel better to get out. The closer I got to the big red door of that honky-tonk, the more energy I felt, and soon, I was standing inside the door and looking around. It seemed like so long since I had been there and even though there were a couple of new faces, all the people I knew came up and either shook my hand, hugged me, or took their hat off as they said hello. I realized they were just paying their respects to me, but it was nice to have the attention. I really felt their love and I felt like I deserved it after what I had been through since my baby's death. I silently ate it up, not realizing then that I was actually getting an odd pleasure out of the comforting sympathy people had for me. Looking back at my life from heaven, I can see now that this, among many other lessons in my life, was not one of the best lessons I should have learned.

I had already figured Payton would be there when I got there. It was still early in the year and the fields of corn were barely out of the ground, let alone close to the point of harvest, so there wasn't much in the way of supplies for moonshine. Besides, Payton had already told me that he felt he was getting too old for running shine. He had been thinking about settling down, learning a trade, and in fact, had already been talking to a man near Atlanta about being a pipe fitter. The job paid well, and would be a useful thing to know, no matter if he stayed in Clayton County or not. I found him sitting at the usual table with Jimbo and some other guys. They were all smoking and drinking, and there was a game of cards going on. I could tell it was a betting game and a couple of their faces told me their hands were not the best ones they had ever been dealt. I just stood beside Payton, with his serious "I'm gonna win this hand" look. He did have a good hand, but it wasn't *that* good. This was a game of bluff and all the years of talking his way out of trouble with the law had made Payton very good at bluffing. The room was almost dead silent as, one by one, the players folded. It was down to two of them and the other guy was sweating. Payton knew he had the upper hand and his cool, calm composure was too much for the other guy. The man folded with two queens and two tens. Payton got a really big grin on his face when he folded over his hand. A pair of twos and a pair of fives. The crowd that had gathered around the table started hootin' and hollerin' and poking fun at the man who folded first. Payton just looked up at me and smiled.

"Hello, Gail. Glad you could make it! It sure took you long enough."

We ended up sitting at a table for the rest of the night as we talked about the past, the present, and he even mentioned the future.

"Gail, I told you before, I am getting too old for this running around. It ain't fun anymore, and I am ready to make a change in my life. What would you think about me being a pipe fitter?"

"Fine with me. As long as I get a set of pretty lace curtains out of the deal."

He chuckled. "How 'bout a window to hang 'em in?"

I looked at him and smiled, thinking about the plans I had made with Max, even if they had been in my mind.

"I would like that very much."

"OK then, it's a deal. You get your pretty lace curtains and a window to hang them in, and I will get dinner for me every day when I get home from work."

We spent that afternoon together and every other afternoon following.

For the next two years, we were almost inseparable. Payton did go to work as a pipe fitter, just as he promised, and I went to work learning how to cook. I was in the kitchen all the time with Mama learning everything she knew, and even creating some new things for the menu as I went. I learned how to make good meals out of almost nothing, and before I knew it, I was one of the best cooks in the county.

Even Jimbo finally admitted he was getting tired of the running around, and soon opted to let the younger boys carry it on their own. Oh, he still dabbled a bit here and there, but he, too, had other interests in mind. He had started talking to Mr. Jones, who made uniform shirts in East Point, about a steadier "more presentable" job. Jimbo also had his eye on one of the ladies he had met at the soda fountain in town and was seriously thinking about settling down. The two of them were looking at a little house near the airport where they would, hopefully, be able to spend the rest of their lives together.

Jimbo, along with my daddy, had also gotten tied into the local chapter of the Ku Klux Klan. That, we found out, was why they would be gone for days. Mama never like Daddy going off like he did, because most of the household responsibilities were now on her to handle. Mama was just thankful for having us kids now that we were all grown enough to help with all the chores that needed to be done.

I turned 21 years old in January of 1943 and on Valentine's Day, Payton made sure he came to see me when Daddy and Mama were both home. He was all dressed up in clothes that I knew weren't his, but I didn't care because he looked so dapper standing there at the bottom of the steps.

"Gail Leighann Martin! Come to the door, please, and bring your folks."

My folks weren't the only onlookers he had. There were six other kids hanging out all over the place, some of them giggling, and the older, more mature girls wearing big smiles at what they anticipated was going to be very romantic. My daddy seemed to know what Payton was up to, but was not going to make it at all easy on him.

"Boy, you look a might uncomfortable in those Sunday best shoes. What you raising a ruckus about?"

Payton grabbed the shirt collar and pulled out on it so he could swallow.

"Mr. Martin, I aim to marry your daughter, and I am asking for her hand in marriage."

Daddy pulled his hat off his head and wrapped his arms around his belly as he leaned on the corner of the house. Daddy looked at Payton, then looked at me, and put his hat back on his head. Walking away from the scene, he chuckled and said, "Yeah, I guess." Daddy was a man of few words, and that was just how he should have been.

"Gail Leighann Martin, this is Valentine's Day, and I can't live without you any longer. Will you accept this sweetheart pin as a token of my love for you? I want to get married as soon as the crops are harvested in the fall and I won't take 'no' for an answer."

Payton stayed for dinner that evening and had many more dinners with us after that night. On November 23, 1943, at a justice of the peace in Fulton County, Georgia, Payton and I were married, just like he said—right after the final harvest in the fall. Payton had another surprise for me. His job as a pipe fitter had turned out to be very good paying and he had saved enough money to buy the land across the street from my mama and daddy. In the months to come, we decided that since I wasn't going to be running moonshine anymore, I would not need my car and the old truck Payton had been driving was pretty shot, so, with Jimbo's permission, we decided to sell my Ford Coupe and his truck. With some of that money Payton bought a better truck and used the rest to buy lumber. He, Daddy, Stan and even Brother, who had come home in between terms of his service, built a house in the tuft of trees across the road, just for me and

Payton to live in. It was *real* nice! It had a bathroom, two bedrooms, a living room/dining room combination that had a half bar that separated the kitchen from the rest of the area. And, just as I was promised, I had my pretty, white lace curtains! Payton made sure I had the best of everything. He was still the provider I knew he would be so many years ago. Now, I truly *did* have it all.

Payton held good to his word about the curtains and I held to mine about dinner every night when he got home. Every weekend, we would spend time with my family, and then we would go out to the honky-tonk and dance! Oh, how I still loved to dance! I didn't think things could get any better for the first year that we were married. That was until Christmas of 1944, when I found out I was pregnant. Horrors flashed in my mind as I remembered the last time I was pregnant. *No!* I told myself. *Things are different now! This time I KNOW who the daddy is and HE knows he is the daddy!* It was at dinner that I broke the news to him. As I told him, I was cautiously looking for some negative reaction on his face. Instead, I saw a glow on his face and he lit up like fireflies in July! He was excited indeed! For the rest of the summer, Payton and I were so much in love and he did everything he could to make sure I was comfortable. On September 19, 1945, the blessed event finally came and Patricia Leighann Sanders came into the world. You, my oldest daughter, were beautiful, just like Addy Mae was, with a head full of curly hair, and the most perfect skin! You were the prettiest little baby Payton and I had ever seen, and the first thing out of your daddy's mouth was, "I want to call her Patti Cake."

So, Patti Cake was your name from then on. Thanks to you, Patti Cake, my life with Payton was now perfect. We had a wonderful life, with a beautiful home, and a beautiful little girl to call "ours." For the next two years life was full. Since we were across the street from Mama and Daddy, my brothers and sisters would get together as often as we could. Most of them had gotten married in the last couple of years, and soon, they, too, had started families of their own, ending up with quite a bunch of people. We had so much fun sitting around that old black pot as the women cooked up chitterlings and fried up fresh pork skins while the men folk took turns cranking that old wooden ice-cream maker until it wouldn't turn anymore. Just knowing how that milk, sugar, and vanilla flavoring was gonna taste was the only good thing about that chore, but since everyone took their turn, it wasn't so bad.

Then, after all of us were full as ticks, we would sit around listening to The Grand Old Opry on the radio Payton had bought for me. To me those seemed like the best of times. With a baby at home, I wasn't able to get out and dance like I used to, so I would just sit in that rocking chair with you in my arms, rocking to the tempo of Roy Acuff's "Walbash Cannon Ball," or The Carter Family as they sang one of my favorite songs, "Will the Circle Be Unbroken." I don't think I ever laughed as hard as I did the first time I heard Minnie Pearl scream "HHOOWWDDYY!" When Grandpa Jones got his banjo goin', Mama would get her a set of spoons, and I would get my harmonica out and we would try our best to keep up. Mostly we just had fun trying, and it helped keep my mind from wandering when I would get a bit restless. Every time I looked at my little girl in my arms, I thought about my younger days, and *sometimes*, I would think back on my days at the honky-tonk. Sometimes I would be deep in thought and Payton would come up and kiss me on the cheek.

"Penny for your thoughts?"

I would smile, and tell him I was just thinking about how happy I was with everything I had. Still, *sometimes* I did miss dancing. Even still, for the next two years, we were the perfect couple.

In June of 1947, I found I was pregnant again, and Payton was happy as a lark!

"Two babies!" he would brag to his friends, and soon we were making plans for the second impending angel.

We were all together, as always, for Thanksgiving and Christmas, and everyone was excited to have another baby in the family. But just after my birthday, I started feeling a little odd. I thought maybe I had just overdone it during the holidays, but soon I started having pains that only a woman who has given birth can understand. Not even a week after celebrating my 26th birthday, I went into labor, and, on January 9, 1948, Maria Diane Sanders was born, earlier than expected and very small. So small, in fact, that we would hold her in one hand and feed her with an eye dropper. It didn't matter. Payton couldn't have been more proud as looked at this new little baby in my arms.

"Gail, she looks a dot in your hand, just as snug as a bug in a rug. That's what her name's gonna be."

So, "Dottie Bug" became your name.

# Chapter Seven
## 'Til Death Do Us Part

FOR THE NEXT YEAR, OR SO, the world thought we were the happiest family they ever saw. I say "thought" because no one ever knew what evil was brewing. Having a baby requires a lot of attention, but having an inquisitive two-year-old as well as a newborn who needed special care required even more attention, and it was all I could do to keep up. Mama offered help when she could, but Daddy's tomato fields still needed tending and since most of my brothers and sisters had grown up, or gotten married and found their own lives required more attention, Mama found herself with limited time. So, for the better part of the day, I would be cleaning up after kids, tending to Dottie Bug, entertaining Patti Cake, washing clothes, cooking, and more frequently, wondering where Payton was staying so long.

Ever since the night he won that card game before we were married, he spent a lot of time at the honky-tonk, drinking and playing cards. He had pretty much stopped hanging out with the guys who delivered the moonshine, choosing instead to be one of their customers. The crowd he hung around now was very much into drinking and card games, and Payton found himself enjoying winning money from them each week. So much that he would rather be with them than come home to his family most days. Oh, he never stopped loving us, especially "his girls." You two were never slighted. When he was home, he would make sure you two had everything you needed and wanted. Patti Cake, you remember spending hours, alone, riding that old rusty tricycle. On one of the rare occasions that his buddies didn't get together for cards on the weekend, he just sat on the front stoop, holding Dottie Bug in his lap, playing with her tiny little fingers and toes, all the while watching you ride around and around, playing alone as if you had a yard full of friends.

The glass of whiskey in his hand was not far from the bottle that filled it, and the more he sat there sipping, the calmer he became. He knew how much you loved that rusty little bike, but he wanted you to have a new one, so he came up with an idea. When it was time for dinner, you parked your little bike next to the tree like it was your own shiny new Coupe. As I saw you walk away from it, glancing back at it over your shoulder with a smile, you reminded me so much of myself when I was 16 years old, looking over my shoulder at the car Jimbo had bought for me to help them with their moonshine runs. I knew right then, even at four years old, that you were going to be a chip off the old block. After dinner, your daddy put you to bed while I fed Dottie Bug and got her ready for bed, then he went outside for what I thought was his evening drink and a smoke.

The next morning, when you went out to ride your tricycle and it wasn't there, I looked at him, with his best poker face on, and felt like he was up to something, but since he never let on, I, too, had assumed someone had stolen it. He helped you look all over the place for it, and even held you as you cried when it was nowhere to be found. Over the next couple of months, you had gotten used to not having it, but I would not trade a million dollars for the look on your face that Christmas morning when you opened the door to see your little tricycle sitting on the front porch, the rust all gone, and painted bright red. Nothing Payton had done before, or since, ever made me as proud of him. It was truly a surprise to you, and I was never any more sure of the love he had for his kids.

No, the love for his children was never a problem. I don't know if it was because he was so much older than me, or because I was so much younger than him, but lately, he had not trusted me much. I never understood it, because I didn't have time for anything but dirty diapers, and snotty noses, and laundry, but, for some reason, he was getting very insecure about our marriage. It could have been his drinking, or it could have been the fact that I was alone a lot lately, and he knew that my womanly desires would rear their ugly head at times. With two kids to tend to, and my mother living across the road, there was not much I could have done to fulfill them, so, when I could, I would just sit and listen to the radio that Payton bought for me and rock one or both of you little girls while I listened to the songs on the radio. I thought back on the days when I could drink and dance—a life I was missing so much. Yet, in my heart I knew I had made my bed, I had to lie in it. I would daydream for a while, but would come back to reality when Dottie Bug would cry, or Patti Cake would want something to eat. Only thing that bothered me was that Payton was out doing the very things I wanted to do, and a bit of resentment would build up.

By the time he would manage his way home, he would be drunk and in no shape to make love to me anymore, which added to my frustrations. We started to argue more and more, and the arguments would frequently result in something in the house being broken, and eventually even times when he would raise his hand to me.

"WHY DON'T YOU LET ME BE? I AIN'T HURTIN' NO ONE, AND I DON'T HAVE TO LISTEN TO THIS NAGGIN'!"

The slurring words would sicken me as they came from his lips.

"I DON'T WANT TO WORK ALL WEEK AND HAVE

TO COME HOME TO A WOMAN WHO HAS NOTHING ELSE TO DO ALL DAY BUT WORRY ABOUT HAVING SEX! WHY DO I EVEN COME HOME ANYMORE?"

It wasn't always that bad. Sometimes it was worse. Mama would hear the fights, and come by the next day, offering her "advice." Her advice was most often along the lines of "a woman's place is to take care of her husband," or "you make sure you hold on to him." As I looked at my mother, I wondered how many times she had been through this same scenario. I knew my daddy could be mean, but we never saw any violence like I was seeing. I wondered if my mama even really knew what I was going through. She sat, looking horrified, as I explained to her about the night before, when Payton had gotten upset over what I had cooked for dinner. I told her how we argued and how he had picked up the dinner table and flipped it like a quarter. I showed her the scar on Patti Cake's face from the piece of shattered tea glass and how this wasn't the first time I had been worried about his fits of anger. Then, a few nights later, I found that my mama must have realized how serious things were, and she had told my daddy about it.

That evening, Daddy drove into the yard and, never turning off the engine, got out, knocked on the door, and told me to make sure to keep my babies in the back room that night.

"Why is that, Daddy? What's going on?"

"Just do as I say, Gail Leighann Martin. Do as I say."

Here again, he used my full name, so it must be serious. My daddy was a man of few words, and he had said all he was going to say. He got back in his truck and left the yard.

Oddly, Payton had come home from the bar early, around 10:00 p.m., because Mr. Johnson, the owner of the bar, had a meeting to go to that evening and many of the patrons were going to attend. Your daddy had been home just long enough to eat dinner and was sitting on the front stoop drinking his whiskey and smoking. When, all of a sudden, he heard ruckus coming down the street and the yard filled up with trucks and cars. The meeting Mr. Johnson was attending was actually a KKK rally, and

Payton was the guest of honor. The trucks and cars pulled in the yard and out jumped men of various sizes, all wearing sheets over their heads. Payton could tell who some of them were because of the cars and trucks they drove, but, nevertheless, the whole scene took his whiskey filled mind by surprise.

At first, he got a grin on his face because he thought they were on their way to visit one of the black families in the area, or maybe some of the Jewish families who had started up businesses in town. When he saw them pulling into the yard, he watched with disbelief as the men in white sheets jumped out of their vehicles and ran towards him. Your daddy stood up and turned to run back up the steps toward the front door but was grabbed by three of the men and thrown to the ground, his glass and bottle of whiskey flying from his hand and bursting against the house. Each of the men were yelling at him, "YOU THINK YOURSELF A BIG STRONG MAN, DO YA?"

"YOU FEEL LIKE A REAL MAN HITTING ON YOUR WOMAN AND KIDS?"

"WE'LL SEE HOW MUCH OF A MAN YOU ARE!"

With those words ringing in his ear, he took one, then another, foot to his stomach, and then he was yanked to a standing position. The wind knocked out of him, he was jerked around and thrown back and forth by several of the men. All of them yelling and cursing at him. Your daddy was completely dazed and shaken up, as he heard them yelling over and over, "PICK ON SOMEONE YOUR OWN SIZE! HIT US LIKE YOU HIT YOUR WIFE!"

"YOU AIN'T SUCH A BIG MAN NOW! COME ON!"

Over and over, he was punched in the stomach, kicked as he fell and made to stand back up to "take it like a man." As soon as I heard the commotion, my daddy's words came back to me. He was telling me not to let my little girls see what was going to happen. It was too late, though, because before I could do anything, Patti Cake was already standing at the front door, screaming not to hurt her daddy.

"STOP IT! STOP IT! YOU'RE HURTING HIM! MAMA, MAKE THEM STOP!"

By that time, several of them had tied together some lumber in the shape of a cross, soaked it in kerosene, and had stood it up right in the middle of the front yard. I squatted down in the doorway, holding on to my four-year-old Patti Cake while two-year-old Dottie Bug was screaming in the living room window, and I watched the whole thing happen. Across the road, I saw my mama standing in the yard by the mailbox. A tear came to my eye as I saw my mama fold her arms in front of her, pulling the green knitted sweater around her chest, then turn and walk back to the house. She knew, as I well as I knew, that this was the way of the Old South.

Finally, the kicking and screaming and cursing was over, and they sat Payton on the ground in front of the burning cross so he could watch as the flames engulfed the cross. That scene was burned into my memory forever, and I thought about it the rest of my days. I wanted to run to him and make things OK, but I thought back to how I felt as he was hitting me, and remembered how cold the linoleum floor felt against my face every time he got drunk. I couldn't move for the longest. I wanted him to know what punishment felt like. It was you, Patti Cake, who finally broke me from my stare. The trucks and cars were gone from the yard and the loud sound of wood burning was all I could hear until your cries to help your daddy came to my ear. I set you two on the front porch, walked over to your daddy and kneeled beside him. He was covered with red dust from the clay ground he had been thrown into so many times, blood flowing from his nose and lower lip.

He looked up at me through swollen eyes as I licked the corner of my apron and wiped his forehead, trying not to make his wounds bleed any worse than they were. I reached behind him, untied the loose knots in the rope that bound his hands, and instinctively wrapped my arms around him as he leaned his bloody face into my chest. I honestly felt sorry for him, but deep inside, I was hoping tonight's visit would change things. Dottie Bug stood there, her young mind too scared to do anything but cry, and Patti Cake lay next to him, crying, rubbing her daddy's leg, telling him she was sorry. For what, I did not know. A few minutes later, my mama came over and helped me get Payton back into the house. She took you girls into the back room while I washed Payton up and got him ready for a much-needed night of rest. She walked into the living room, looked at Payton sleeping on the couch, gave me a hug, and without saying a word about what happened, walked out the door and across the street. I went to close the door and noticed that my daddy's truck was home. I wondered again if this would teach your daddy a lesson. I was soon to find out.

The cross burning was never mentioned in the family, even though I knew everyone knew about it. It was a major embarrassment for me and wasn't the kind of thing that was talked about around the table. Only once did anyone in the family ask me about my home life again. Fearing I might get another cross in the yard, I lied and hid the real truth. In any event, it must have affected his pride more than his intelligence because it was only a couple of weeks before he started drinking again. First he would sneak around and drink behind my back for fear of me telling on him. Then, he stopped hiding it at all. Instead, the drinking got worse. So did the gambling. He started missing work, and he would be gone for days at a time, never once offering me an explanation. Each time he came home, I would end up defending myself against the things he thought I was doing. After he would leave the next day, I would nurse my wounds. Wounds that ranged from hurt feelings to black eyes, big bruises and even a dislocated shoulder.

I was hanging his clean shirts on the line to dry when I broke down and cried. I was listening to Patti Cake and Dottie Bug playing and heard one of them talking mean to each other. I fell to my knees right there in the back yard and decided I could not take it anymore. His anger and his drinking had finally affected his children and I had to do something about it. I didn't want my children to see me crying, so I stood up, finished hanging the clothes as though nothing was wrong, and I decided I needed a drink. So I found one of the whiskey bottles Payton had hidden and sat on the stoop. As I poured a mason jar half full, I raised the glass in the air, toasted my kids, and downed it in one long swallow.

The rest of the afternoon, I didn't do much of anything but play with my little girls in the yard. I taught you how to use lids for plates, sticks for forks and knives, and I even showed you how to use rocks and blocks to make your own house. We had fun that day, and it was the best day I remembered having in years. It was getting late in the afternoon, so I went in the house to start dinner. Payton had come home straight from work but he only stayed long enough to change clothes and eat. There was a big poker game going on, and there was supposed to be a lot of money to be won in the game. Your Aunt Lacy Jane's husband, Ted, his brother Jeff, who, as you know is your Aunt Frannie's husband, their brother Chris, and another of their friends named Davey James were all supposed to be playing for a pool of around five hundred dollars. The three brothers-in-law had come up with a plan to win the other man's money by cheating.

Payton was sure he was going to win because "None of them know how to play a good game of poker." I knew that Jeff wasn't much good at cards, but I didn't know about his brother's Ted or Chris, or that other man, Davey. I had only heard them talk about him, but I had never met him. I wasn't very worried about the money or the game, I was just working my brain hard as I could to figure out how I was going to stop the violence when he came home. I prayed over and over for God to grant me the strength to get through the night, and to help me keep this from happening again. I walked him to the door and, as he left, I stood there watching as he walked across the drive and turned towards Flat Shoals Road. I turned and went in to the kitchen to clean up from dinner. I rinsed the big iron skillet I had used to fry the chicken and placed it in the dish drainer while I was listening to the sounds of young voices playing. Never was there a sweeter sound than my babies, as Patti Cake tried to teach her little sister how to use the box of crayons their Granny Sanders had bought them. I didn't realize that night what an important role Payton's mother would play in our life, and soon, very soon.

I had finally gotten you both in bed and realized how very tired I was. It was unusually nice and quiet, almost tranquil, in the house that night. I sat at the dining table, sipped on another glass of whiskey from yet another bottle I had found hidden around the house, and lit myself a cigarette. I let my mind go blank for a minute as the whiskey relaxed my mind, then I started thinking. The guest list at my pity party included Maxwell Jackson, Payton, Addy Mae, Mama and Daddy, and even my Patti Cake and Dottie Bug. I cried, I smiled, and cried some more, until I realized that having my daddy burn a cross in the front yard didn't get to him, so I would have to get to him myself. Life was never going to change as long as I was afraid to stand up to him myself. I raised my glass towards the door and offered a toast to that oddly tranquil night.

"Tonight, the disrespect ends! Tonight, I am going to teach him a lesson! After tonight, there won't be any more playing cards with his buddies and God only knows what else he stays involved in. I have warned him I couldn't take it anymore, and now I am not playing."

It was shortly after midnight when I heard him walking up the steps to the kitchen door. I had been sitting for several hours waiting on him, and I just knew he was going to be drunk and ready to fight. I had downed just enough whiskey to relax me, and had already gotten myself all geared up to discussing matters as soon as he got home. I had already decided everything I was going to tell him but I knew I needed to catch him off-guard if I was going to get him to listen. So I grabbed the first thing I could find—that heavy cast iron pan I had fried his chicken in for dinner. I thought about how much taller he was than me, so I pulled the chair up beside the door and stood there, both arms clinching the heavy, black cast iron skillet. *The bastard's gonna be sorry he left me here alone again, and even sorrier if he's drunk!* My adrenaline was flowing so quickly in my veins that I had no idea how heavy that cast iron pan truly was. That is, until he opened the door and I swung it at him. As he entered through the doorway, he was kind of slumped over, and I thought, *This poor drunk bastard can hardly stand up!* Even if he had seen the pan coming at him, he could not have ducked fast enough, and I hit him with all the strength I could muster for my 135-pound frame. I hit him square on the back of the head and stood there on that chair, looking as, in seemingly slow motion, he fell to the floor, his face hitting hard against the same cold vinyl I had felt so many times before.

I stood there with that frying pan held over my head, waiting to swing it one more time, if I needed to. Maybe it was a few seconds, maybe it was a few minutes, I am not sure, but I realized he wasn't moving. I watched his shirt to make sure he was still breathing and I noticed a large red mark on the side of his face. I knew immediately I hadn't put it there, so he must have been hurt when he came home. Suddenly, my arms realized how heavy that pan was and, almost unconsciously, I stepped off the chair, walked over to the sink, rinsed the pan off and placed it back on the dish drainer next to the sink. I walked over to your daddy and as I kneeled down, I saw the puddle of blood gathering under his head and I panicked. I jumped up, ran screaming out the door, and over to get my daddy.

"DADDY! DADDY! PAYTON IS HURT REAL BAD! PLEASE COME HELP! HE'S IN THE KITCHEN ON THE FLOOR! I CAN'T GO BACK OVER THERE!"

He and Mama grabbed a jacket and started back towards the house. Mama had to practically drag me with her, but Daddy walked right in the kitchen and over to where your daddy lay.

"What happened to him?" was all my daddy said as he scooped him up like a child, and hurriedly carried him out the door and across the road, putting him down in the back of his truck. Mama stayed behind to look after you girls and I crawled in the back of the truck, sitting next to your daddy. I sat and looked at him, praying he would be all right, wondering if he was going to die. When we got to Crawford Long Hospital, the nurses took him into one of the rooms while the ward clerk asked me some questions. I lied as I explained how he had come home and had barely opened the door when he fell to the floor. *It isn't a complete lie,* I told myself. I just left out the part about me hitting him with a frying pan. I didn't know if I could ever tell anyone that. The doctor that night told us he was in a coma, and though things didn't look very good for him, they would do all they could to help him.

Your granddaddy waited with me long enough for them to get him in a room and asked if I wanted a ride home.

"No, Daddy, I am gonna stay with Payton. I want to make sure he is OK. Just ask Mama to watch the girls for me, please."

What I really wanted to do was make sure that if Payton woke up, I was there to make sure he didn't tell anyone what I had done.

"You get some rest," he said. "You're gonna need your strength."

He hugged me like a father should, but all the while I had a sneaky feeling he was wanting to ask me what I did to my husband. I slept in the room with him that night, and each night afterwards. I would sit and watch him breathe, watching for his chest to rise and fall, all the while thinking, *What have I done? What will I do if he dies?* Then, an even more serious thought came to my mind. *What if he lives? What will I do then?*

I was torn up inside, but the people around me thought I was being the loving wife. No one knew I was mentally tormenting myself, preparing myself to be charged with murder. For the next week, my sisters took turns helping watch you girls so my mama could keep up the daily chores, and one or more of them would come by the hospital to make sure I was all right, too. Ellie visited me more than anyone else, and she was the one to tell that they had found the guys that beat up Payton.

"WHAT?" I was flabbergasted!

"Yeah, the police think Lacy Jane's husband, Ted, his brother Chris and that other man, Davey James, caused it. They had arrested Jeff, too, but couldn't get enough proof that he had anything to do with it, so they let him go. They all had a big fight during the card game and it got out of hand. One of them accused the other of cheating and one blow led to another. Before you know it, Payton was in the middle of it and they all beat the tar out of him."

This was too much for me to take! I knew it wasn't true, but I didn't say anything. That was the moment I decided I could never tell anyone about the frying pan. This was my chance to get away with it. For all anyone knew, the fight was how he got hurt and since no one was asking me anything about how it happened, maybe I was in the clear. All I needed to do was keep my mouth shut. And, so I did. For the rest of my life. But, I never stopped thinking about it from that day forward. It was my cross to bear, and I bore it 'til I died. I promise you that!

"Gail, how long has it been since you ate? You look horrible! Why don't you go down to the cafeteria and get something to eat?" Your Uncle Allen said as he gave me a couple of dollars and a cigarette.

I had been sitting with your daddy for the past eight days, and barely anything but crackers to eat. I was so torn up inside between worrying that he would live or die and the worrying about my two little girls. I wished I could just go home and forget any of this had happened, but I knew it was all too real and I had to go through it. Reluctantly, I took Allen's money and headed toward the cafeteria. I stood there in front of the food, but nothing seemed to look appetizing, so I grabbed a moon pie and an RC Cola. No sooner had I bit into that stale little cookie and lit a cigarette, when Ellie came running into the room.

"Gail, you need to come back to the room! Payton's just died."

That day, April 24, 1950, at Crawford Long Hospital, in downtown Atlanta, barely 5 miles from where Payton and I were married, a 36-year-old father of two left the earth, forever changing the life I had grown to know, and so began the molding of my life, and the lives of my two daughters.

There was a lot of paperwork to complete, and signing the documents as they were put in front of me was very hard, but it was nothing compared to the events that took place over the next few months. When Payton's mother was informed that her son had been taken to the hospital and that he may not live, she was not at all calm. It is not normal for a parent to outlive their child, and she was sure that foul play was afoot. She had not been present at the hospital very often during the week as I sat and watched her son breathe, but it wasn't because she wasn't interested. Instead, she was busy trying to get to the bottom of what had happened the night her son was taken to the hospital.

Having recently been through the death of his father, she was already a strong woman, and had accepted that her son would probably not come home alive. Payton's sister, Florence Jean, tagged along to make sure her mother was OK as she spent a lot of time with the authorities from Fulton and Clayton counties, making sure they never slacked up on the investigation. Her intent was to find the person responsible and she even hired a private investigator of her own to check behind the county investigators. But rest assured, her presence was well known the day after he died.

That evening, I finally went home and I wanted nothing more than to hold my little girls. It was the first time in over a week since I had seen you, and I wondered how I could ever tell you that your daddy had gone to heaven. I just wanted to take a bath and sleep, but all I did was lay there, thinking about what I had done. I wondered if the fight had killed him, or if I had done it. I wondered what everyone else thought. I wondered about the investigation my mother-in-law was spearheading. *What have they found out? What do they know? Would they think one of the other guys did it?* Ellie told me they had all been arrested, pending investigation, but could I live with that? Should I say anything? I felt as if I had just lay down when I heard you, Patti Cake, getting Dottie Bug out of bed before heading to the living room. You were both so glad to see me when you got up and I kneeled down and held you with all my might. Patti Cake, you were asking about your daddy and I didn't know what to say.

"Mama, when is Daddy coming home? I miss him, and Dottie Bug misses him, too. Where have you been for so long? Is Daddy here, too?"

It tore my heart out, and I could find no words to express to you that your daddy was not going to be coming home. When you started crying, Dottie Bug, by instinct, started crying, too, and soon all of us were balling our eyes out. That's when the big police car pulled up, and I knew why they were there. In my heart, I had known all along that Payton's mother would leave no stone unturned, and she was not leaving anyone out of the investigation.

The sheriff was a large man, bigger than anyone I had seen around here before. He and I spoke for a few minutes and he explained why he was there.

"Ms. Sanders, I am afraid you have to come with me. I have a court order requesting your presence at the station to discuss the evening of April 16, 1950. You are not under arrest, at this time, but I have been informed to place your daughters in the care of their grandmother, a Mrs. Martha Jean Sanders, until such time a hearing can prove you fit to care for your children. Please gather their things so we can be on our way."

I tried to hold back the horror I was feeling at that very moment. *They aren't charging me with murder,* I thought. *They only want to question me. It might still turn out alright as long as I watch what I say. Mrs. Sanders will watch my children for me. It will all be OK.* I gathered some things for the both of you to wear, and the sheriff and I carried you to the car. He held the door as I put you both in the back seat and made sure you were seated good. Both of you were crying and it was all I could do to keep my composure. I was just as scared as you were, but I was hoping for the best. As we pulled up to the curb at your Granny Sanders' house, she and "Aunt Flo," as folks called her, were waiting at the fence, as if they had been expecting us for a while. Neither said much to me as I took you each out of the car and sat you on the curb. You were both still crying as I asked Aunt Flo to take care of my babies.

"They'll be fine with us," she said, very matter-of-factly.

I felt a strong sense of judgment coming from both of them, and though your grandmother didn't speak to me, her eyes said it all. The sheriff opened the door once again, and I got in. Only this time he opened the rear door for me to enter. As he drove away from that house on Tanner Road, the last thing I saw was my little Patti Cake jumping from her granny's arms and running down the street, collapsing on the road behind us crying. That sight was another of the visions that burned in my mind every day, and another guilt I carried with me until I died.

# Chapter Eight
## *My First Real Job*

I SPENT THE NEXT FEW DAYS answering questions over and over again about my marriage, his friends, his drinking, and his moonshine days. The detectives came at me, one by one, each leaving the room with no more information that when he first entered.

"Did you know of any reason why he would be murdered?"
"Did you have a reason to kill him?"
"What happened that night?"

I had made up my mind that they thought it was someone else's wrongdoing, and I had tried to point the finger at the man I did not know.

"It had to be Davey James, no one around here knew much about him," I told them and soon I had almost convinced myself.

They wanted it to be me so badly that I could smell it on them, but I never quivered, never broke my story. I held to the tale of my husband coming home from a game of cards. I told them all that I had lay down across the bed after putting my babies down for the night. I was insistent that I was awakened by the sound of my husband beating on the kitchen door, and how he fell to the ground as I opened it; that I was thinking he might have just had too much to drink. I told them about the trip to the hospital that evening and sitting vigil, all the while worrying about my babies. Yes, I had all of them convinced I was innocent.

Well, almost all of them. There was one man not so easily snookered. His name was well known around Clayton, Fulton, and even Fayette counties. Howard Sylvester had made a name for himself as being the best at what he did. Your Granny Sanders had "made arrangements" with the district attorney's office to have him on the case. It was as if she had it out for me, because she had all of her fingers pointing to me. Anyways, whenever he took on a case everyone knew he was going to win, and the defending attorneys were scared to go up against him in court. But this time he had run into brick walls on every side of his investigations, and nothing concrete could be found to prosecute me. Not willing to admit defeat, he went after the rest of the suspects for the murder, and all he was able to get me with was a ruling by the Department of Family and Children Services that I must be able to provide a healthy, happy home for my children before I could be allowed to act as sole custodian.

In other words, he was able to take my babies from me until I could find a job paying enough money to support ya'll. I was even served with papers that said I could not come near you for a period of one year, unless I had found suitable work. To make things worse, because of a restraining order, I was not even allowed to attend the funeral, and just so she could make sure I was not able to attend, your Granny Sanders had the ceremony at her house. I did get one piece of satisfaction, though. Just like with your sister Addy Mae, because your daddy did not belong to the church, the elders would not allow him to be buried in the plots with the rest of the family. Since I was married to him, they made sure it was up to me to decide where to bury him. Against her strongest demands, they agreed to bury your daddy next to the little girl who everyone had come to assume was his. Your

Granny Sanders tried her best, but the elders stood firm to their decision, and your daddy was laid to rest next to my first little baby, Addy Mae. Old Mrs. Sanders was furious, swearing that she would never have anything to do with putting a gravestone over her son that would mark for eternity such a desecration to her family name. And she held to that statement. From that moment until the day she died, she never had anything good to say to me again.

After they could not hold me accountable for Payton's death, and they turned their attentions to the other men in the card game that night, I was so busy trying to find work so I could get my babies back that I had not even thought about my sister Lacy Jane and her family. I had not once been to visit her, and I had purposely stayed away from the jail where Ted, Chris and Davey James were being held for a murder they most likely didn't commit. Then, one day I was at Ellie's house when Lacey Jane came by on her way to visit your Uncle Ted.

My heart sank as I watched them drive up and noticed that Lacy Jane almost didn't get out once she saw I was there. My mind told me she was going to be mad at me when she finally came in, but instead I was greeted by huge tears in her eyes as she immediately began apologizing for what had happened. The guilt in me got worse and worse as Lacy Jane told me how the trials were going, and that it now looked like it would be months before the trials were over. His lawyer was not very optimistic and he was trying as hard as he could to change the verdict from murder, which would get a death penalty, to second degree murder, which would bring only a life sentence if found guilty. With every word from her lips, my heart sank lower and lower in my chest. I had to leave. I made up an excuse and headed for the door. Ellie stopped me in the kitchen and asked if I was OK. I just couldn't look at her or Lacy anymore.

I headed my car towards Roosevelt Highway. I didn't know where I would end up, but suddenly I was feeling lower than I ever felt in my life. I stopped at a soda shop in Hapeville known for making the best cherry lime sours anyone ever had. Every time I went, I felt like a little girl, all over again, and I needed so badly to feel good about something for a change. As I sat there, looking around at the large glass jars of pills, and the white-and-black checked floors, I had a sudden urge to ask the lady if she needed any help and to my surprise, she accepted, telling me she would love the help. As we talked, she told me that her husband was the pharmacist and they had owned the business for some time. They had gotten very popular in recent months, especially the soda fountain, and the two of them had been discussing hiring someone just that morning.

"You came along at a perfect time, Gail! I am glad to have you on board! Can you start in the morning?"

I accepted and spent the next few weeks learning how to make ice-cream floats, banana splits, and those wonderful cherry lime sours. I quickly became known by the men in town, too! I got real big tips from a few of them, and I realized that I still had what the boys liked. There was one man in particular who took extra effort to speak to me. He said he liked my smile, and he would spend more than enough time sitting on the stools in front of me. By the time he had finished playing with his ice-cream soda, it was mostly melted and looked more like bananas and cherries in a glass of chocolate milk. When he asked if I had a boyfriend, my mind raced through all kinds of answers. I thought about my babies but realized that this had nothing to do with ya'll, and it wasn't going to hurt you at all by my being a woman. I thought about Payton, but then I remembered I was a widower. So with that coy little grin I was known for so many years ago, I batted my eyes at him and honestly told him, "No, I don't. Would you like to be my boyfriend?"

Oh, how easily it all came back to me. I was really getting into this. I told him what time I got off, and we met at Thompson's Café around the corner when I left the soda shop. It turned out that he was married, so I decided it might not be in my best interest to carry on with him, so I broke it off. He never came back in the shop again, but I felt better about myself, and he ended up not being the only man I entertained. Soon I had the soda fountain hopping with suitors.

The owners, though they were happy for the business, soon felt that the soda business traffic was almost hindering the regular shoppers from their everyday needs. So when one of the men came to me offering an opportunity to learn a trade, the owners were almost relieved when I jumped at the chance. My couple of months dishing out ice-cream soda had paid off. I was offered an opportunity to learn welding for Fulton Wrought Iron and I finally had the opportunity I needed to get my babies back! Nearly eight months after you were taken away, I was finally able to go to Howard Sylvester's office and tell him I had a job now.

"Ms. Martin, just because you have a job, doesn't mean you can have your children back. You have to prove to the courts that you can provide for them. From what I understand, soda shop cashiers don't make a lot of money, So, unless you can do more of your fast talking to a judge, you can rest assured you are not quite back in the saddle."

Upset, but holding my composure, through gritted teeth I said, "Mr. Sylvester, I don't know who you are getting your information from, but they are quite behind the times. I'll have you know that I have learned a good trade. I am now making a lot of money making wrought iron railings. I might not be able to support them today, but it is only going to be a couple of weeks before I will prove you and old Mrs. Sanders completely wrong!"

Not wanting me to have the last word, he ended the conversation with, "We'll see about that. I have always suspected you had more to do with the death of your husband than you are letting on about. I might not be able to prove it now but the case will stay on my desk until I die before I admit defeat."

Then he grabbed me by the elbow and escorted me out of the room, slamming the door behind me.

"Damn, he's mean!" I said, as I walked out the front door to the truck Payton had driven before he died.

I sat in the truck, thinking about my conversation with Mr. Sylvester, when I suddenly got a whiff of Payton's scent. I opened the window and let some air in but it didn't help. I was soon fighting the urge to unswallow, just like the first night I snuck out to go to honky-tonk and just like the day Maxwell Jackson's grandmother dropped the bomb on me when I was thirteen. All the way home, I felt like he was in the truck with me. By the time I got home, I was panic-stricken, and I immediately went to the kitchen, pulled a water pail and some cleanser from under the sink. I started scrubbing the floor in front of the kitchen door and at that very moment, I wanted to get rid of anything that had to do with Payton.

    I scrubbed and scrubbed until my knuckles were bleeding and I was crying. I lay there on the kitchen floor, missing my babies, and wishing I could take back the past four months. I wish I could go back to the night I told my mother about your daddy's fit in the kitchen. If I could, she would not have told my daddy, and the cross would not have been burned in the yard, and, Payton would not have been mad at me, and we would still be a family. I fell asleep, curled up like a baby by the kitchen table. That night I learned another of the lessons that haunted me the rest of my life. "Be careful what you ask for, you just might get it."

# Chapter Nine
## *104 Lee Street*

IN THE WEEKS SINCE I HAD cried myself to sleep just feet away from the spot where your daddy lay bleeding, I spent as much time as I could working. I saved as much of my money as I could, and since I didn't have a banking account, I would fold money in little squares and find hiding places in my purse, or in books or magazines. I was determined that I was going to get my children back, but I was even more determined to prove to old Mrs. Sanders and that horrible Mr. Sylvester that I was fit to be a mother. All the while, through my brother and sisters and my mama, Lacy Jane began reaching out to me more than ever. She kept telling everyone how much it was costing her for the attorney, and how hard it was to feed her kids. I avoided contact with her, and, as guilty as it made me feel, I let her believe it was because I was upset that her husband might be involved in the murder of your daddy. I could not afford to have anything upset my plans.

I had been working at Fulton Wrought Iron for over three

months already, but it felt like years since I was able to see my two babies. Then, one day I came home to find a letter in the mailbox from an attorney's office. When I opened it, I could barely make out what it was saying, so I took it across the road to see if Daddy could tell me what it meant. It was from a lawyer representing an insurance company. It seems that your daddy had taken out an insurance policy for a good deal of money. *Even in death*, I thought, *he is still the provider I knew he would be those many years ago*. I had to make an appointment to see them "at my earliest convenience" so they could discuss the amount of money I was to receive. The letter did not state exactly how much I was to receive, but, in my head, I immediately started spending the money. I took a good look around the house Payton, my brothers, and my daddy had built for me and I realized just how much of Payton was still there.

I walked from room to room and memories from the past few years came to me as if they were just happening. I could almost see my Patti Cake and Dottie Bug sleeping in their little bed. I could remember the nights of passion and plain good sex in the room across the hall from them. I walked into the kitchen and could almost smell the bacon frying for the big breakfasts I would cook your daddy before he went to work; or the beans and cornbread that was waiting for him when he got home. Then I got sick at my stomach as I looked over at the vinyl floor by the kitchen door, and could still see the puddle of blood as it pooled around his head. Suddenly, the room filled with his scent, just as the truck had as I left Mr. Sylvester's office. I went outside and sat on the front door step, lit up a cigarette, and poured a glass of whiskey from another one of the bottles I had found in one of your daddy's hiding places. I sat there, finishing my second glass, and the smell of burning wood came to my mind, bringing with the night that cross burned in front of me and my little girls. I knew the first thing I had to do was get out of that house. But, *how?*

Daddy and Stan took me into town to meet with the insurance company. Daddy did most of the talking, and Stan mostly held my hand while they talked and I had to give the man written approval for my daddy to discuss the matter. I could not tell which of the four of us was the most uncomfortable talking about the murder, especially since the persons involved were family members. We finally made it through the details and he told me I was to receive a check in the amount of $5,000.

"FIVE THOUSAND DOLLARS? IS THAT ALL?" I yelled out as Stan grabbed me on the hand and squeezed.

"Mrs. Sanders, the insurance policy your husband had was one of our most basic policies. It is customarily intended for burial purposes, and most beneficiaries find it very adequate for burial expenses."

"Well, I bet none of them have been through what I am going through. That isn't going to be enough to take care of everything I need to take care of."

The stout little man looked flustered as he continued, "I am sorry, Mrs. Sanders, but there is nothing more we can do. The policy holder was informed of all payouts when he signed for the policy."

I suppose Daddy and Stan were afraid I was getting too riled up, because they both rose from their chairs about the same time and politely thanked the man behind the desk as they ushered me out the door.

On the way home, I was sitting in between Daddy and Stan with my chin propped on my knee. The wheels in my mind were turning faster than the wheels on Daddy's old pickup truck. *How am I gonna get my kids back and myself away from the past on five thousand dollars?* I didn't know if I had thought it to myself, or if I had said it out loud. Daddy drove me by Fulton Wrought Iron to get my paycheck and on the way home he took us through College Park. I looked at the houses and saw several "for sale" signs on the front of them, and I asked Daddy about the prices.

"I want to give my babies a fresh start when they come home," I explained to them. "I just don't think I can bear to live in that house any more because there are too many bad memories."

"What's wrong with the one you got?" Daddy asked, in his frugal manner. "It's paid for, ain't it? You got no need for no other house."

The conversation was immediately dismissed but I kept thinking about it. I had a hunch that it was going to be the right move for me, but I had to do some more figuring on my finances. That night I added up everything I had—a check for $5000, $300 I had stuffed "here and there" and the paycheck that I had just gotten. I put it all in an envelope and slipped it under the pillow I was lying on. That night I dreamed about driving to Riverdale and picking up my little girls from your grandmother's house and taking ya'll home to our new house. I slept good that night, not one bad dream, and when I woke up, I was at peace with things for a change.

I had made my plan and I had something to look forward to, so for the next month or so, I would work all day, then drive by the neighborhoods in College Park to look at houses. However, I didn't get quite the cooperation I thought I was going to get. I went to house after house to talk to the owners, but each time I found them unwilling, even scared to talk to me. Then I finally realized the problem. I went home one evening, frustrated because I had not gotten anywhere in my looking. I stood in front of the bathroom mirror, running a hand through my sooty hair when I heard a voice telling me to look at myself. When it finally hit me, I started laughing hysterically.

Suddenly, I could see why no one wanted to talk to me. Instead of the strawberry hair and coy grin I had been able to flaunt all my life, I was covered head to toe with the black soot from the iron I molded, and I must have really been a sight with the big white circles around my eyes where my safety glasses were all day. So I decided I would wait until the weekends and go looking. I had already made up my mind that I wanted to live in that neighborhood, and I went every weekend, looking at every house that was for sale in the area until I found a place.

The house had not been lived in at all and, in fact, had never even been finished and most people would have driven right on past it because of the condition. There was a man in the front yard of the house looking as though he might be cleaning it up a bit so I stopped to talk for a minute. He was Mr. Rivers, the real estate man, and as we talked, I found that the owner had been in construction for several years and had bought the house thinking he would be able to work on it a little at a time until he finished it. Before he had the house ready to move in, he had gotten a job with the Corps of Engineers building Lake Allatoona, up near Cartersville, and finishing the house turned out to be more than he could do alone. Since the area around the lake promised to be a great place to live, he was thinking about moving up that way and had pretty much lost interest in finishing it.

"Besides," Mr. Rivers explained, "his wife never liked this area of town anyway."

As I looked around the yard and inside the house, I saw potential. It was similar to the one your daddy built for me, but it was obvious that it was never taken care of. Even still, I decided it could be a nice home, with a little love.

"How much is it?"

"Well, since he wants to get rid of it, but wants to get back at least the money he'd spent, he would let her go for seven thousand dollars."

I thought about the seven thousand dollars and knew I was a bit short, but I knew what my mama always said, "Where there is a will, there is a way," and I decided I wanted that house. I also decide it was time I began to take advantage of some of the contacts I had made when I was working at the soda fountain. Mr. Perkins was the president of the bank on the other side of the railroad tracks from the drugstore. He had been one of my favorite customers, not because of the size of the tips, but because he talked to me like an adult. There was never any pressure in our conversations, and he always took the time to ask about my family. I felt comfortable with him and he was one of the few people who ever knew about the events of my life, well, *most* of the events anyway. Mr. Perkins always said he could sit and listen to my stories all day long. I even told him that my mother-in-law had custody of my babies until I could prove I could provide for my children.

Of course, I never told him about Howard Sylvester, and how he was determined to prove I was guilty of murdering my husband. I had gotten good at telling people what I thought they needed to know, and, as you can both attest, I held that ability until the day I died. That Monday I asked my boss if I could take a day off, explaining that I was going to see the bank about a loan, and was thankful when he agreed. I had been working there long enough to have some vacation time saved up, so I took off the following Thursday and Friday. So far, everything was falling into place, as if it were meant to be. I spent the next two days looking through the magazines and books I had put money in, and searched every crease and fold of my pocket book to get all my money together. I was ready to put it all down on the house that would reunite me and my babies.

I went into the bank as soon as they opened and was able to see Mr. Perkins almost immediately. I had the insurance check for $5,000 and the money I had saved up and to my surprise, getting my loan was easier than I ever expected. By lunchtime, I was the proud owner of not just a loan for the $7,000 for the house, but he had coordinated everything with Mr. Rivers' real estate company so I could buy the house. Mr. Perkins told me about savings accounts and checking accounts, and he opened one of each using the money I had with me that morning. Yes, Mr. Perkins was my angel that day because I now had everything I needed to prove to your grandmother and Mr. Sylvester that I could provide for you both. I was the happiest I had ever been. The first thing I did when I left that afternoon was go to the Department of Family and Children's Services and talk to them. I showed them all the paperwork, and I signed all kinds of documents. I left there very proud of myself and everything I had accomplished; wanting nothing more than to see Mama and Daddy to tell them the good news!

Your Aunt Frannie was already there when I pulled up and was just as excited as I was about my new house. Of course,

Daddy, being Daddy, complained that I didn't need to move, and threw phrases like "Throwing money out the window!" and "Running from your problems!" He was determined that I was making a big mistake, but was lost for argument when Frannie said she would love to move closer to Mama and Daddy. For quite some time she and your Uncle Jeff had been talking about moving closer to the family, and this was the perfect opportunity for them to do so, and for me to get rid of the house.

Daddy's only reply to that was, "Well, at least I didn't waste my time building that house. I guess that's OK."

I was now even more determined that this was all meant to be. I wanted so badly to get away from the guilt I felt every time I went in that house that the next day, Jeff, Frannie, and I were talking to a lawyer to have the deed to the house transferred. For most of the day, we purposely avoided mentioning anything that happened to me and my family over the past few months, taking care to talk mostly of how excited their three kids would be to live across the street from their grandparents. Of course Lacey Jane, and how hard life was for her, eventually came up, and every mention of them made the guilt in me rage stronger. I just changed the subject because I wasn't going to let anything bring me down from the joy of knowing that I was so very close to getting my girls back.

Within two weeks I had moved away from that spot in the kitchen floor, sold Payton's old truck to a guy from work, and contacted Children's Services and made arrangements to get my babies back. I had even taken part of the money I had saved and bought myself an old Ford coupe; similar to the one I had driven in my moonshine days. Only this one was bright yellow! I called it "The Yellow Canary" and I just knew I was hot as I drove through town! I drove through Hapeville, College Park, down Roosevelt Highway—anywhere I thought I might see someone I knew. I had the world on a string that day and I was very much enjoying all the looks and attention I got as I threw my famous coy grin around at all the men as they watched me drive by everywhere I went.

As the workweek ended, my anticipation grew stronger and I watched the clock more each minute. Despite your grandmother's and Mr. Sylvester's arguments against it, Children's Services decided that I had provided ample proof to them that I could, indeed, provide for my children. I had to sign documents stating that I intended on fixing the things that were wrong with the house, and I had to have my boss sign a document that I was eligible for long-term employment with the company, but once the various documents were completed, the next step was to go and pick up my babies.

I was nervous about seeing your grandmother, and I was even nervous about seeing ya'll, but the closer I got to the house you two had been living in for most of the last year, the more violated I felt, and the angrier I got. I was determined not to cause any problems, so while your Aunt Flo took you two out for a walk, I sat patiently while your grandmother had a few words with me. I never expected a warm welcome from her, but I didn't expect the lecture I got from her either. She went on and on about how much you two meant to her, and accusingly let me know how disappointed she was that nothing was ever done to me. She, just like Mr. Sylvester, had decided all along that I had been the one to kill your daddy. She made sure she kept telling me how happy the two of you had been with her and how much you had enjoyed living in a warm, beautiful home. Even though the words cut me like razor blades, I never let it show. I maintained my composure as I kept asking her to bring me my babies, purposely not showing that I was boiling inside.

If your Aunt Flo had not brought you in when she did, I may have been in trouble again, but as soon as the door opened and you two ran into the room, all the anger I had simply disappeared and was replaced with the same love I had every time I saw you from that day forward. Never in my life had anything brought me as much joy as that very second. Watching you come running across that living room floor with your arms out, screaming, "MAMA! MAMA!" I knew at that very moment that blood was, indeed, thicker than water, and as I kneeled down in front of my two babies, wrapping my arms around you both, I looked up at your grandmother and flashed a coy grin at her. She looked as if she had been slapped in the face, so sure I would not be greeted well as I stood up and the two of you held onto my legs like you would never let go. Old Mrs. Sanders, her arms folded across the chest she had puffed out in anger, had decided she was not through telling me what she thought.

"Gail Martin, I never thought you good enough for my son, and the only reason I accepted you was because of my son. I can't say that I am saddened to see you leave this house, but I am sorry to see you leave with my grandchildren!"

She followed us to the car, all the while giving me a piece of her mind. I remember muttering something about her being an "Old Hen" as I put you girls in the back seat. I was picking up the little suitcase that your grandmother had put your things in, as she continued, "It will be a cold day in Hell before I forget what you have done! You may think me an old hen now but you will think me a rooster when I finish flogging you for what I know is the truth!"

I had listened to enough of her tongue lashing, and as I opened the car door to the get in, I looked her in the eye, curled my arm up to flex the muscle I had developed molding wrought iron, smiled, and said, "Well, you old rooster, hop up on here and crow!"

I got in the car, slammed the door, looked her in the face, lit a cigarette, and drove off to our new home at 104 Lee Street.

# Chapter Ten
## *Misguided by Flesh*

I COULD NOT HAVE BEEN HAPPIER. I had a job, a house, a car, and I had my babies back! I had turned over a new leaf in life, and was going to do everything I could to be the best mother anyone could imagine. I even had money enough to hire someone to watch my children while I worked all day. I had asked some of the neighbors about babysitters, and had gone through a couple of different girls, always ending up firing them for one reason or another. I was very thankful when I came across Jewel, a very proud Cherokee Indian woman, who I was certain an angel sent to help me. Through Jewel, I learned a lot about humility, and she seemed to know me better than even I did.

Jewel taught me a lot about faith, and self-healing, and even taught me how to "talk the fire" from wounds, and allow them to heal without scars. She reassured me that God still loved me, regardless of the decisions of my past. Through her, I regained the faith in God that my mama had tried so hard to instill in me, and I started taking the three of us to church again, and every

Sunday we would get up early and go to Sunday school to learn the lessons of the Lord. I knew people were probably talking about me, but I was not worried about their judgments. I was doing what I could to get forgiveness from the Lord. I kept hoping that sharing the power of the Lord with my family and friends was an opportunity for me to start lessening that burden on my heart and in my mind. For the longest time, I was faithful to my goal, but I was fighting hard against the urges of my past; urges which eventually reclaimed my mind and body.

In the past year your Uncle Ted, his brother Chris, and Davey James had all been convicted of various charges and each were placed in prison to carry out their sentences. Though I maintained my innocence in public, the horrible guilt boiled in me every day. Slowly I had made amends with Lacey Jane, and volunteered to help her out by taking her food each week. I even started making a special trip each Sunday morning to take her and her kids to church, then back home again. Yes, I was trying in my own way to apologize for what happened to her husband and the others, but I could never bring myself to tell the truth. Perhaps I might have saved my brother-in-law from going to prison. I would think to myself, *What would happen to my babies? I would die without them!* So I kept my mouth shut, and just did all I could for my sister and her kids. Everyone thought I was being so forgiving. I just didn't have the heart to tell anyone, so I never did. Like so many other secrets, I took that to my grave.

As the months and years passed, I found myself daydreaming once again. They were the same daydreams I had when I was married to Payton. I would listen to the music on the radio as Kitty Wells sang, "It Wasn't God Who Made Honky Tonk Angels" directly to me. I just knew she was talking about me, and I felt even guiltier. Mostly I felt guilty about your daddy lying there in that grave next to your sister Addy Mae. I had been so mad at his mother over the words she had spoken to me, and I had tried so hard to forget all the events of that tragic part of my life. Then, for some reason, one morning I woke up and decided I was going to put some closure to it all.

I was sure that if I fulfilled my obligations to your daddy that things would get better for me, so I went to the hardware store and bought a bag of cement. I used one of my bread pans and mixed up enough cement to make two gravestones, one for your daddy, and one for your sister. Patti Cake, you were with me when I was doing it and I remember you asking what it was for. I told you it was to put on the ground above your daddy, and you watched me make each one of them. You even went with me to the gravesite, and stood there as I put them on the ground above them. Afterwards, I felt better, and my conscious eased a bit, because I had finally finished what I was supposed to do.

Later that evening, I asked Jewel to watch the two of you, making up some story about where I had to go that night. I did this several times in the weeks and months to follow, always ending up at some honky-tonk, or other bar, but always, searching for some man to show me the attention I needed to make me feel wanted. I never hurt anyone, and I never stopped going to church, but the flirty feelings I had never went away. Instead, they just got stronger as I continued to look for something to make me happy. This went on for almost three years before I found that someone. It happened quite by accident at a drive-in restaurant on Roosevelt Highway. I know you both remember it, because it was the first time either of you ever ate fast food. His name was John Lewis Wyatt. Yes, it was the man you two came to know as your stepfather for so many years. Meeting your stepfather was the first time in such a long time that I had met someone who made me feel like I wanted to feel.

I had heard your daddy talking about him, and I had seen him at family functions several years ago, but then he was only a kid. He definitely wasn't a child anymore! He was very much a man, and a very good-looking man at that! He hadn't long been home from the Navy, and had just turned 18 barely two weeks before, so a couple of his brothers and some of his friends had taken him out to celebrate. They had been drinking all afternoon and decided they wanted something to eat. It was purely a coincidence that we all ended up at that drive-in at the same time but I was not complaining. It was, I guess, love at first sight for both of us, and he came over and leaned in the passenger side window. We knew it would be awkward because of the family relationship, but we decided that being related by marriage should not stop us from getting to know each other. I leaned over the seat and made a place for you, Patti Cake, to sit in the back next to your sister. Johnny got in, and as you two ate the burger and fries, he and I talked. Before I knew what was happening, the chemistry between us took over and we had our hands all over each other.

It was getting late, and it wasn't long before you two fell asleep in the back seat, which was for the best, because it allowed me and Johnny to get "further along." In fact, we got so much "further along" that he helped me get the two of you in the house and off to bed. He wasn't the first man I had brought into the house at 104 Lee Street since we moved in, but he was the first to spend the night, and the first man I ever wanted to bring back. Johnny decided it would be best that he leave before you two got up. Besides, he was determined to get a job at the airport and wanted to be there early the next morning anyway, so he got up before you two even knew he was there. He had been going there every day for the past two weeks, working on his own time, just to prove to them he was worth hiring. I had never heard of anyone else doing that, and I decided then that this man was going to make something of his self one day.

I had thoughts of him maybe becoming a pilot, or something, and us being able to travel. I liked that thought, and I didn't want to miss out on the chance. The next night he came to dinner after you two went to bed, but like the day before, he left before you got up. This went on for the next few weeks, and when they finally offered him a job there, he asked me to marry him. Six weeks after meeting Johnny, I was married again. Johnny did his best to treat you girls like his own and Dottie Bug seemed to enjoy the piggyback rides Johnny gave the two of you, but you, Patti Cake, were the hardest to win over. You still remembered your daddy, and you never quite let go of those memories.

*This time*, I would told myself, *I will love, honor, and obey him for the rest of my life.* It was a promise I kept, and a promise that, eventually, almost cost me my family. Johnny and I were newlyweds, and both of us wanted very much to be with each other, though neither of you were old enough to understand the feelings he and I had. I made certain vows when I married him, and I was only doing what I thought I was supposed to do. I loved him. Looking back on things, I can see now how you might have felt neglected, but it was very hard for me to spread myself between my husband and my two children, and I never intended to hurt either one of you. Instead, I always wanted your lives to be as normal as they could be.

It's just that with Johnny working the hours he did at the airport, and being home during the day, he needed the rest. Sending you outside for such long periods of time allowed me to spend time with him as a wife, and allowed him time to rest before going off to work. I checked on you all the time, for a while, but each time I saw you, you were playing so well together that I never knew you were having problems coping with my life with your stepfather. That, I have to admit, is when I started taking the two of you for granted. I ended up spending more and more time with Johnny, and Johnny expected more and more time from me. I was so wrapped up in the feelings I had for him that all I could think about was being with him. He made me feel wanted for the first time in many years and I couldn't wait to leave work to be with him. I even came to take Mr. and Mrs. Craig for granted once I knew they were willing to feed the two of you. I never worried about you as long as I knew you were over at Brenda and Andrew's house. They were such nice people, and the time you spent there gave me the opportunity to spend time being Johnny's wife.

I was honoring him. When Johnny's work shifts started changing each week, it got too much for me to work and still take him back and forth to work, so he told me to quit my job so I could take care of him. I enjoyed getting up each morning to cook his breakfast, and I was glad to make him lunch every day. I never minded making dinner for him and I never once got upset about getting up at two o'clock in the morning to take him something to eat. The way I looked at it, it was just a chance to spend time with him. I also didn't know I was doing the two of you an injustice by making you clean the house. Johnny said you were both old enough to have chores.

"It won't hurt either of them to have chores!" he would tell me. "You just worry about taking care of your husband!"

I obeyed him. Whenever I didn't do what he told me to do, he got upset, and the way he would pout and turn me away really bothered me. I had never felt such a cold and lonely feeling as I did when he would be mad at me. I wanted him to love me so much that I would do anything for him. I was getting older now and had been lonely for far too long before he came along. I came to understand how your daddy might have felt because I knew that a younger man was desirable to younger women and I knew I would have to work harder to keep him. Even though I think he also knew I was still a very desirable woman, too, because every time we would go out in public men would smile at me. I quickly learned to control my coy little grin because it would make him crazy with jealousy. To keep Johnny happy, eventually we stopped going out in public at all.

One weekend I made the mistake of telling him about someone I had met before him. It turns out he knew the guy, and he must have known he was a rounder. He got so upset about my having had relations with his friend that we got in an argument about how many men I knew before him. I already told you he was a jealous man, and I just couldn't make him understand that I was not seeing anyone else; or that he was the only man I wanted to be with. Soon I even stopped going to church with you girls because he was so sure I was meeting other men there, and Johnny made me believe that the elders of the church would find it kind of strange that I would marry my husband's blood relative.

"Talk like that spreads fast," Johnny would tell me. "I don't want no one knowing my business. I think it best that if you just 'have' to go, then you should go to a different church."

He even had me convinced that children belonged in church

so the adults could sleep in on Sundays, so I would get the two of you ready and walk you up the street to the church Johnny told me to take you to. Johnny had me believing that he knew best. I only wanted to keep the peace around the house, so I did as I was told. I never liked it when Johnny was upset with me. I never wanted him not to want me.

# Chapter Eleven
## *We All Run from Something*

MARRIED PEOPLE WHO ARE HONEST WITH each other know things about each other that the rest of the world doesn't. Johnny and I were the exception. Even though he knew more about me than any other person, and there wasn't much I didn't know about him, the exception was that Johnny never knew just how his cousin had died. He had heard stories in the family; he had even heard the stories that passed around the town. One day he confronted me about them and I let him tell me what he had been hearing. It seemed that everyone had his or her own story and it helped me out in the end because he didn't know what to believe. Once again, I had to withhold the truth, and all the years of guilt came running into my head and heart, but I told him the same story I told the police. I told him I heard Payton beating on the door, and watched as he fell on the floor, the puddle of blood pooling around his head. I couldn't take a chance on him leaving me because of what happened, so I let him believe that Davey James, Chris, and your Uncle Ted were in jail because of it. He seemed to buy that story, and that was the story I stuck to.

Two years after I married Johnny, I found I was going to have a baby. I didn't tell him about because I was scared he wouldn't want it, so I did something that I know God punished me for in later years. I wasn't a spring chicken like I used to be, and though it was only a month or two into the pregnancy, I was already having problems keeping up with him. I didn't have the energy to run down to the lake or the river fishing, and I wanted to be with him so badly, so I decided I would get rid of it. I had heard from one of the girls at the soda shop several years back that she had taken a coat hanger to herself to get rid of her accidental pregnancy. When I heard it, I thought how horrible it sounded, but I was so afraid I was going to lose Johnny that I decided to take a coat hanger to myself while he was at work. I had no idea how I was supposed to do it, and, even though I did lose the baby, I bled so much that I got infected and almost lost my life. I had been running a fever for a couple of days after that and when I passed out right in front of him, he took me to the hospital; scared he was going to lose me.

I had to tell him about losing the baby that night, but I was too scared to tell him I did this to myself. Instead, I lied and told him I was going to let the baby be a surprise, and I apologized for not being able to carry it, but he said he wanted to try again. My lie kept him from being upset and I found out just how much he loved me when he bought me a St. Christopher necklace, telling me it would keep me safe from harm. I never took that necklace off. For weeks afterwards, I would rub the necklace between my thumb and fingers, praying that Johnny would forgive me for what I had done. But more importantly, I prayed that God would forgive me. I promised I would be there "through good times and bad, through sickness and health," so I accepted what life brought me. I just didn't expect it to be that bad in the end.

In a few months, I found out I was going to have another baby, and at first, Johnny was proud that he was finally going to have a child of his own. However, as time passed, and I couldn't have sex with him anymore, he got very distant. I felt that God was maybe punishing me for being less of a wife to Johnny because I couldn't keep up with his manly desires. After all, I was in my 30s by then, and not the young, energetic woman I was when I married him. I did my best to keep up as much as possible, but then, just like when your daddy would get depressed, Johnny started drinking. It started when we would play cards, or when his family would come over and visit. I know neither of you liked his family much, and to tell you the truth, I wasn't too fond of them either, but I was his wife, and I tried to be as good as my word. There I was—full-blown pregnant, big as a barn, and he was still a young, good-looking man. I kept going as long as I could, but it wasn't until after your sister Jenny was born that he paid me much attention.

Then, when Jenny developed meningitis, I didn't have time to worry about much else. I know I put a huge burden on the two of you, but I needed your help, and I didn't mean to forget you. The two of you always had each other, and there were times I felt like an outsider in your life. I never realized that the reason you left me out was because you felt like I left you out. I never liked how Johnny talked to you, but Jenny was our child, too, and she needed special attention. I was only trying to be the wife Johnny wanted, and a good mother to Jenny.

Since leaving the welding job when Johnny and I first got married, Johnny and I had spent most of the money I had saved. Johnny and I spent it, a little at a time, going fishing, or drinking, and soon all we had was his income so we had to give up some things and cut back on some expenses. He started spending a lot of money on liquor and the money problems got worse. So, to keep us going, I had managed to work a couple of small jobs to help buy food, gas, and groceries, but each time, Johnny would tell me that "a woman's place was in the home, taking care of kids." So each time I would quit my job and stay home. But it wasn't the kids I ended up taking care of.

While the two of you did your daily chores, I tried to get keep my marriage together by catering to him. He was ignoring me for days at a time, always mad at something, or one of the kids, and he would be rude to my family, sometimes not even talking to them when they came by. I would usually make up some excuse about him being tired, or not feeling well, but eventually they got so uncomfortable that they quit coming by at all. Looking back on it all, I just wish he had not been so mean to my children. He would yell and tell me that my two kids treated his child differently and that the two of you needed discipline. I just knew that as long as Johnny was happy, he wasn't mean to me, so I spent a lot of my time trying to make things OK with him. In between being a mother to Jenny, and a wife to Johnny, I didn't have a lot of time for the two of you. I came to accept his drinking, because, even though he would get deathly sick from it, it never got in the way of his working. I would just make sure he was up and ready in plenty of time for me to get him to work, and later I would gladly run him something to eat.

He never understood why, despite all our efforts, despite how many times I would call him your daddy, the two of you would never call him daddy, or why neither of you ever wanted to do what he said. Patti Cake, you in particular could get under his skin quicker than anyone he knew, and since he was always afraid of you, I think that is why he stopped me from letting you go around your Granny Sanders. He knew how much you loved visiting her, but every time you were around her, you came back more determined that he wasn't your father and that he wasn't going to tell you what to do, and he would end up whooping you just to show you he could. For years this went on, and when one of you would ask about your granny, all I could think of was, "Hush! Don't let your daddy hear you talking about that!"

I knew he would be mad and all, so I kept your daddy's name from coming up as much as possible.

Then the time came when you, Patti Cake, started liking boys. Johnny did not want to lose control of either of you, and when you met Wayne, Johnny knew there was going to be trouble. That is why he kept you from seeing him as long as he could. It irritated the devil out of him to see you happy for some reason, and when you deliberately went against his wishes, it made him madder than a hornet. I will never forget the night he and I got in a fight because I was defending my little Patti Cake about being with Wayne. I can remember it like it was yesterday, that pretty blouse I had on, and those green corduroy slacks. That night, I was hoping he might think me pretty, too. Unfortunately, it turned out that I didn't get much of a chance to look pretty and I missed the days when I used to get compliments, or smiles, or even looks from other men. I was so proud of how good I looked that day, and I felt so good about life that I felt as if I could defend the world.

When he started cussing about you seeing boys, all it took was for me to say one thing in your defense, and he showed me just what he felt about me. He picked me up like a rag doll, and squeezed me so hard I thought he was going to kill me. If it hadn't been for you, Patti Cake, coming in when you did, with that knife in your hand, he might have just done it. I never hurt so bad as when I felt my ribs cracking under the pressure of his drunken squeeze. I was very thankful when it was over, I just hated it that my children had to see it. God was definitely with us all that night and I was very thankful that Chuck was home when you called and able to come and get you as fast as he did. How on earth, little Dottie Bug, you ever knew to pull that firing pin out of the shotgun, I will never know, but if it hadn't been for you, one of us would have been shot that very night. If my daddy hadn't been home, it would have been Johnny to die by Chuck's hand. That night I honestly feared Johnny, and I learned never to sass him again.

That is also why I was grateful when I was told that you, Patti Cake, were going to move out and get married. That fight between Wayne and Johnny really scared me, and for everyone's sake, I thought it was best that I let you leave, so I was more than happy to sign the papers to let you get married. Besides by then, Johnny had started drinking so much that it didn't take much to make him angry. Having you around only made things harder for me to keep the peace. I kept telling myself, *Things will be better when she is married and I won't have to worry about her anymore.* It never occurred to me that he would turn towards Dottie Bug for his entertainment and for the next year or so, it was just me and Johnny, and little Jenny and Dottie Bug.

Dottie Bug, you were growing into quite a good-looking woman yourself, but I always worried about you. You had the prettiest smile, and your figure was really filling out. When I was your age, I was flaunting my figure all over the place, but Dottie Bug, you seldom smiled, and you never held her shoulders back. You always wore sweaters, or big clothes, and I would have to remind you all the time to stand up straight, or hold your chin up so I could see your pretty face. I thought that you were getting along with Johnny so much better now that your older sister was out of the house. Sure, he whipped you when he felt like you needed it, even though sometimes I didn't see any reason for it, but you started to always obey him; you never seemed to sass him like Patti Cake had, and he seemed to enjoy being around you much more than he ever did Patti Cake. He, too, knew you were becoming a woman, and he used to laugh and kid you about your "little green apples." But, Dottie Bug, *never*, in a million *years*, could I have been prepared for the conversation Johnny and I had just before you were about to start the eight grade. I was, after all, his wife, and even if I *was* in my late thirties and starting to get some age on me, and even though he *was* much younger, I was still proud of myself. I thought I looked in good shape for a woman my age with three children.

He had been drinking a lot that night. In fact, he started before he even left the airport good. It was usual to stop at the corner store there to get a fifth of liquor, and it was usual for him to start drinking it before he got home. What worried me that night was how he sat in the car and opened that bottle of Jack Daniels whiskey, chugged it down like it was sweet tea, then went back in for another. He opened it, took another swig, placed it between his legs, and told me he needed to get home so he could talk to me. Evidently, he had been thinking about it all day at work, and nothing was going to do but for him to tell me. When we got home, and he ate the dinner I made for him, he finished off the bottle he had bought and huge tears came into his eyes. I felt so sorry for him at that very minute, but that minute passed quickly.

I almost fell in the floor when he told me that he was not interested in me anymore, and that he had eyes for another woman. But that wasn't the worst of it. You could have knocked me over with a feather when he told me that he had fallen in love with my very own daughter! Yes, Dottie Bug, he confessed an undying love for you in the very kitchen that I had just made dinner for him! I felt an anger in my soul that I had not felt since the night I knew your daddy was going to come home drunk! I looked around and saw a frying pan sitting on the stove, and for a second I had the urge to hit him in the head with it just like I had done to your daddy before!

Instead, I thought about Lacey Jane and her kids. I thought about losing you and Patti Cake to your grandmother. Then I thought about that horrible Mr. Sylvester and his promise to watch for me to make a mistake until the day he died. I didn't know what to say. I was crushed! I started cursing at him, throwing dishes and angry words. We argued for hours over what he had told me, but as I sat on the kitchen chair, tired from the arguing and fighting, I looked at him, his sad face, words slurring from his drunken lips, and remembered my promise. "For better or worse, for richer or poorer." I also thought about what I had done over the years, and my life flashed before me. The baby I had bore—from which man I didn't know; the lies I told about my husband's death; all the men I had carried on with, and the family I had turned my back on. Then, the thought came to my mind, *This is my cross to bear. This is how God is punishing me. I have made my bed now I have to lie in it.*

The next day, I tried to act as if nothing happened. I hoped against hope that you had not heard any of the argument the night before, and if you had, I hoped you had not heard what the argument was about. For the next four years, until you became Mrs. Robert Monroe, and ran from me like your sister did, I stood by my man, an almost broken woman; catering to a man who told me time and time again that I was older than he was. I knew what was happening between you and him, but never had the courage to talk to you about it. I knew it, but I loved him and he was all I had wanted. I made my choice, and I stuck to it.

After the two of you left, life was a bit better for me and Jenny and Johnny, but his drinking got worse. With his drinking came money problems as well. We got behind on the mortgage payments, and even Mr. Jenkins from the bank couldn't keep us from losing the house. Every time Mr. Jenkins would call, or come by the house, Johnny would either hang up on him, or run him off, so sure I was messing around with him. We ended up moving three times over the next couple of years, each time because of money, and each time because of his drinking. Jenny must have had the same feelings the two of you had, because she ran off and got married just as soon as she turned 15, upset at me for not stepping in after she told me about how Johnny's brother had touched her in places. I just didn't know what to do. I was torn between losing her as I had the two of you, and losing him. I was afraid, mostly of having no one. So I stood good to my word. Actually, I suppose in a way, I, too, ran. I ran my children off.

# Chapter Twelve
## The "Golden" Years

WITH ALL THE CHILDREN GONE, JOHNNY and I finally had a lot of time to spend together. Finally, I didn't have to worry about Johnny and Patti Cake fighting all the time, or wonder what Johnny was doing to Dottie Bug, or even about Jenny and how detached she was from me. Yes, Johnny and I thought we had it all. We were alone; and that was how he always liked it. Finally, I could be Johnny's wife, and Johnny could be my husband. We found new places to spend time, and took full advantage of being alone. For the next few years, we spent a lot of time together just fishing, and playing cards with Johnny's family. I even started visiting my brothers and sisters again for the first time in years. My daddy had died a few years back and my aging mama needed a lot of care, so my brothers and sisters all took turns doing our share to look after her. After all, blood is thicker than water, and, regardless of what happened so many years ago, Mama had raised us to be Christians. Well, we considered ourselves to be anyway.

Johnny's youngest brother was killed at war and left his mama and daddy some money. They bought some land on a lake and decided to divide it up between them and us. It was a completely wooded lot and it took several years to clean off. We worked on it in the evenings, on weekends, and on vacation days he got, and eventually cleared enough space for a house and garden. By now, I was getting older and the alcohol was really taking a toll on Johnny. He fought illnesses all the time now and the one thing the doctors told him he needed was rest, so we decided that fishing might be the best medicine for him. We spent as much time as we could trying out new fishing holes, hitting all the local places, then we heard some people talking about the ocean fishing in Panama City. All it took was one time and we were hooked! We went there as often as possible, many times getting cash from our Mastercharge or Visa. That is when I got good with a checkbook, and I also got real good at borrowing from one credit card to pay another. I had learned over the years that Johnny didn't know how to save a dime, so I started lying to him about money, telling him we had one amount, when we actually had another. When Johnny got paid, I could tell you where every dime was and where it was going. If not for me, we would have not gotten through the years to come.

Johnny and I finally had all the time we always wanted, but there was so much missing in my life. I began to miss my kids more than ever, and the older I got, sometimes I would almost resent the years I had spent in that form of exile. I wanted my little girls back. I finally talked the two of you into visiting, taking care to let you know when Johnny wasn't home so we could talk and gradually over the next few years, you would come and stay for longer and longer periods. Whether because of his illnesses, or his age, or maybe he got tired of my crying all the time, Johnny wore down, and eventually acted more like a father to the two of you. When you finally started calling him "daddy," instead of Johnny, or just "him," you would not believe how proud he was! By then, you both had families of your own, and surprising to everyone, despite how their relationship started, Johnny had taken quite a liking to your husbands, Chuck and Robert.

Once the land had been cleared, and we started planting on it, we spent hours and hours in the gardens and I was never prouder of anything more than the sight of my children and grandchildren taking home bags and boxes of the food Johnny and I had worked so hard to grow, can, and freeze. No one ever left our house without having something to eat, and there was always plenty for the next group. Year after year, God was good enough to let me keep providing, and there was always a buttered biscuit waiting in the oven, or dinner on the stove. Soon there was even a fourth generation to feed, and God still provided for me because I provided for everybody. I have to admit, Johnny and I ended up being much better as grandparents than we ever were as parents. None of the grandchildren ever knew about the past, and in the end, we enjoyed every minute of "our" grandkids coming down to help or to visit.

But the more he enjoyed the camping, and hunting, and just being with the boys, the more I started feeling neglected and left out by him. He also began to read more and more, and that, too, left me feeling isolated. Yes, it is true, I had gained a lot of weight over the years, and I wasn't aging very gracefully at all. It was becoming harder for me to get around, and my health was becoming a major hindrance. Still, in my heart and mind, I wanted to be the woman who he used to love and I didn't like how he could still get around and go almost as he pleased. Feeling left out really bothered me, and I was envious that he could still enjoy life, so I would use my health as an excuse for him not to be able to go as he pleased, but I never intended on it turning into the game that people thought we played. I simply resented getting old and sick. I started insisting that I didn't feel well, and tried my best to make him believe he didn't feel well. Maybe it *was* childish of me, but I had sacrificed a lot for him, and it made me mad that I was being left alone all the time. Maybe there were times when I might have exaggerated, but, after all, I sacrificed a lot for Johnny, and he sometimes acted as if he didn't love me anymore. I was determined not to go through it while he enjoyed life. I gave up too much for him, and I would be damned before I missed out on anything because of him. I would rather us both do without than let him enjoy life without me.

Most people who have been married, at least as long as Johnny and I were, look forward to retirement and living the rest of their lives enjoying what they had made and shared together. In the winter of our lives, when I should have been nothing more than a proud grandmother and Johnny should have been gearing his mind to nothing more than a garden and a fishing pole, my health really took a turn for the worse and I started having panic attacks that only Johnny could stop. Mostly what would bring on the panic attacks was the silence in the house. As I aged, all the years of lies started to crawl into my mind, and I would sometimes hear Mrs. Sanders telling me that she would never forget what I had done.

My mama always told me, "Purdy is as purdy does." I hoped that by being kind to others, God would forgive me, and one day, even Mrs. Sanders might forgive me, too. Sometimes I would even hear Mr. Sylvester laughing at me, and I knew he was still watching me everywhere I went. Sometimes I would see your real daddy, or hear him telling me that my time would be soon. At first, when one of them came to me, all I could do was cry because I was so scared, and Johnny would hold me in his arms until I would feel better. But the older I got, the more frequently my ghosts would visit and more frequently another attack would come up. I would need Johnny to help me through it, so that is why I would call him home from work so many times in the last few years before he retired, but I could never tell him why they happened. I know Johnny probably got tired of the calls, but he never told me no. Perhaps if he had, he would not have resented me so much in our later years.

Yes, the ghosts I lived with became more ominous, and so real to me that I was honestly scared to be by myself. My fear of those ghosts turned me into such a child, and it wasn't long before my family thought I was crazy. Both of you remember how I used to call you and cry for you to come and visit me. Sometimes it was because I was just mad and lonely, but most of the time, it was because of the ghosts. Once again I ran my family away, only this time they all thought I was crazy. I wish now that I had been more honest with everyone. Perhaps those ghosts might not have been so real. Maybe I might not have exaggerated to Johnny about my illness. Maybe, even, I might not have gotten so sick. It is too late to worry about that now, I guess.

    Though few people ever knew it, Johnny and I spent a big part of our later years regretting some of the decisions made all those years before. As our children and grandchildren got older and their own lives required their attention, we were alone, and sometimes it would even feel like old times. But just the two of us playing cards, or watching television, or an occasional visit from one of the kids was not enough to keep us from that resentment that always seemed to seep into our lives. Once Johnny retired and we spent more time alone, we both had a lot of time to talk about the things we did in life. Some things we knew we would one day regret, and some things we would always remember fondly. Johnny and I had spent the first years of our lives trying to be together, and the last years of our lives resenting each other for being that very person we had wanted to be with from the beginning.

    Because of his illnesses, Johnny found himself having to work harder to make love to me until he just couldn't anymore, and he would get irritated by his inability. The frustrations we both felt started causing distance between us. Soon we were bickering back and forth about small things, just like young children do. As age crept into our bodies, and bad health began affecting us both, unfortunately, we let our illnesses consume us. Yet, looking back, despite all the trips to the doctors, all the years of trying to be sicker than the other just to see who got the most attention, we never meant anyone any harm. We were just two sick people who had lost their meaning in life. As for Johnny, well, only the Lord knows what he needed in life. I spent over forty years thinking it was me. I am sure that Johnny spent all those years thinking he was all I needed.

    But as for me, all I ever wanted in life was to feel loved and wanted. In the end, as the final decision time drew nearer, I knew that I needed to be where it all started. How many times I sat in the sun, eyes closed, thinking back on my childhood. I sat for hours poking little pieces of napkin in the wrought iron table, pretending I was planting tomatoes in the fields with my mama, and the way the sun warmed my face always brought back memories of the morning after I married Maxwell Jackson. Even for just a split second, I was thirteen years old again, and sitting on the steps of that country store, enjoying the very first store-bought food I ever had. The breeze off the dirt road around that lake took me back to the smell of the dirt roads under my Yellow Canary as I delivered moonshine. My life was so much simpler then.

Yes, girls, I had lived most of my life regretting things I did when I started my life, and I lived a long time with the ghosts of those decisions. Turns out that I was the happiest in the years I was with your father, and that is where I wanted to be in the end. Patti Cake, Dottie Bug, I hope now you can understand why I acted like I did, and why I made some of the decisions I made. Patti Cake, over the years, I tried to talk to you, as the oldest child, but each time I got up the nerve to confess, it just wasn't the right time.

When you have lived with the kind of truths I had hidden for so many years, there is only one man who can forgive it, and I was so afraid He would not forgive me that I fought hard to hold on to life as long as I could. I had to hear that everyone would be OK. I had to wait until I heard my little brother Stan's voice, "It's OK, Gail. We'll be fine. It's OK to let go."

You both know I am with you still today, more than ever. You also know that I love you with all my heart.

I love, love, love you. You're just my little dahlins! Now, promise you won't let anyone ever forget me.

Printed in the United States
122315LV00005B/144/A